HEARTS
OF ICE

HEARTS OF ICE

Adi Rule

SCHOLASTIC INC.

The publisher does not have any control over and does not assume any responsibility for author or third-party websites or their content.

This book is a work of fiction. Names, characters, places, and incidents are either the product of the author's imagination or are used fictitiously, and any resemblance to actual persons, living or dead, business establishments, events, or locales is entirely coincidental.

ISBN 978-1-338-33274-2

10 9 8 7 6 5 4 3 2 1   19 20 21 22 23

Printed in the U.S.A.   40

First printing 2019

Book design by Yaffa Jaskoll

FOR K

1

There was always an empty seat on the school bus next to Evangeline Reynolds. It wasn't because she was mean, or had a frightening appearance, or because she oozed poison from her pores like an Australian cane toad. No, Evangeline was a kind, plain-looking person with run-of-the-mill pores, which people would have found out if they got to know her. But they never did. She was never around long enough.

Today, Evangeline was the new kid yet again, at Lakecrest Middle School, or was it Crestlake Middle School? She was dressed to fade into the background—her mother didn't like flashy colors. But just in case someone did notice her and decide to sit down, she pushed her gray knapsack under her seat. She pulled her beige coat tightly around herself so it didn't puff over into the other seat. Plenty of room.

Evangeline took out her pencil case and held it next to her ear against the window, where no one could see it very well. "Yes," she said, as though she were talking on a phone (her mother didn't approve of cell phones). "I can teach you all about sword fighting. Come to my house next Tuesday." She glanced at the line of students passing her in the aisle. Nobody cared about sword fighting, apparently. Which was just as well, because in truth, Evangeline couldn't tell a sword from a swordfish—her mother would never have let her learn anything as interesting as that.

"Cookies?" she said into her pencil case, a little more loudly. "Of course. I have cupboards full of homemade cookies. I can't possibly eat them all by myself. I really don't know what I'm going to do."

Again, nobody noticed. Evangeline watched her classmates board the bus, one by one. A girl with blue-striped hair passed by without a second look. A boy wearing a yellow T-shirt that said GOLDFISH CLUB in glitter plopped down next to his friend. Nobody looked at Evangeline and said, "Hi! You're new, right? What's your name?" They all just continued to shuffle by and choose other seats until there was nobody waiting in the parking lot to get on.

Evangeline looked away and put her fingers on the window glass. Her stomach felt icy, shards of coldness that spread through her skin, even though it was a warm May day outside. She had that feeling again—a strange, old feeling that there should be *someone* in that empty seat. Not quite a memory, and not quite a ghost, it was something more like a *space.* On the school bus, at the dinner table, in the darkness of her room at night—Evangeline had always had the peculiar idea that there was someone missing. Someone who would notice her.

The last to board the bus were two girls carrying muddy track shoes. They took the seats across from Evangeline. She caught their eye and they looked over at her curiously.

Evangeline's heart jumped. She smiled and waved. "Hi!"

"Uh—hi," the girl closest to the aisle said, like she thought it might be a trap. "You're Norma Jean, right? The new kid?"

"Evangeline," Evangeline said. "Nice to meet you."

"Okay," the girl said. "Well, I'm Bridget." There was an awkward silence. Evangeline tried frantically to think of something to talk about before the girls went back to ignoring her—if she played sports or had blue hair, or even if she belonged to the Goldfish Club, maybe she'd have something to say. But there was really nothing special about her. Nothing except—

"It's my birthday on Sunday," she blurted. Everyone was special on their birthday, right?

The girls across the aisle laughed. Was that good? "Happy birthday," said the one near the window, the one who wasn't Bridget.

"Thanks." Evangeline swallowed. "Hey—do you want to come to my birthday party?"

She immediately regretted it. Did kids at Crestlake Middle School even have birthday parties, or were they just for babies? Not to mention, Evangeline hadn't actually *asked* if she could have a party, and her mom would say no. Her mom always said no.

But the girls shrugged. "Okay," not-Bridget said. "As long as there's cake."

"There will be!" Evangeline said before she could stop herself.

The girls laughed again. "I'll text you tomorrow, okay?" Bridget said. "What's your number?"

Luckily, Evangeline already had her new number memorized. She pronounced the digits clearly. "It's a landline," she said, a little embarrassed, but they didn't seem to care.

The bus creaked to a stop at a busy corner store and both girls rose to get off. "See you Sunday!" Evangeline called after them. "Bring your friends!"

"Will do. Thanks, Emmaline!"

Evangeline watched them go, her heart still jumping. She pressed her forehead against the cool glass of the bus window.

Bring your friends? Cake? I must be out of my mind, she thought.

But then again, she was turning twelve. She was old enough to make her own choices. Maybe—*maybe*—her mom would let her have this one party this one time. She'd never ask for anything again. She and her mom would probably be gone from Lakecrest before her birthday next year. Bridget and not-Bridget and their friends would never remember her name, even if they ended up ever getting it right. But if she had this one birthday party, then forever after, she would have a memory of smiles and sugar and all the brightest colors.

As the bus groaned to a stop in front of Evangeline's boring, tan house with the boring, scraggly trees out front, she bounced out of her seat, afraid and excited. By the time her feet touched the driveway, it had started to snow glorious, fat flakes. And where her forehead had touched the window, a beautiful spiderweb of frost began to form.

As the snow flurries intensified, Evangeline slid to a stop halfway up the driveway. "Not again!" she said to herself. "Not *now!*" It always seemed to start snowing at the worst possible times, when Evangeline was worried or nervous or excited. And the only thing her mother hated more than flashy colors, cell phones, and birthday parties was snow.

2

"Send the clowns away—I'm home!" Evangeline shouted, bursting through the door into the kitchen. Sometimes she imagined her mother doing the most outrageous things while Evangeline was at school, like adopting twenty-five puppies or heading up a meeting of a secret society of assassins. Today, she imagined her mother dancing all over the house with a group of clown friends. Wild secrets like that would explain why the curtains were always drawn at their house, why she and her mom wore plain clothes and never did anything fun. Secret clown parties and assassinations were far more interesting than the idea that Evangeline's mother was just boring.

"What?" Her mom's voice came from the living room. "Come tell me about your day!"

Evangeline shook the snow out of her jacket and hung it up, dropped her gray backpack onto a kitchen chair, and breezed through the doorway by the magnet-free fridge. The house still smelled like paint. It was a new house, so it hadn't had time to develop any character yet. Evangeline thought her mother probably preferred it that way.

She found her mom on her knees by the sofa amid cardboard moving boxes, unpacking white plates and extracting them one at a time from their newspaper cocoons. Today, Evangeline's mother was wearing jeans and an uninteresting button-down shirt, and her face wore the same calm expression it always did. Like a flat lake.

Her eyes sparkled when she saw Evangeline. "How was school?"

Evangeline sat on the carpet next to her and pulled open a box marked SILVERWARE. "It was—"

"Sweetie, you're covered with snow!" Her mother's head whipped around. She went to the window and pulled back the heavy curtains just a little, letting a beam of light into the dim room. Evangeline's mother peered out with wide, nervous eyes at where the big white flakes were falling.

Evangeline looked down. Sure enough, a little snow had collected on her pants. She should have dusted herself off better.

"It might be slippery out there," her mom said. That was her usual excuse to stay inside whenever there was even a dusting of snow. "I guess I'll go grocery shopping tomorrow instead of this afternoon. You don't mind frozen waffles for dinner, do you?" She gave a laugh, then lifted a stack of plates and headed for the kitchen.

"Frozen waffles are my favorite." Evangeline dropped a fork into her pile of forks with a *clink*. "Maybe we can have them for my birthday on Sunday, too." She was proud of herself for working *birthday* into the conversation. Now for the hard part.

"You're so funny," her mom called from the other room. Her voice was lighter now. "But if you want Eggos on your birthday, that's what we'll do."

Evangeline could hear the clatter of Pyrex as her mom put dishes away. She put her hands on the plastic lid of a tub marked BLANKETS, took a deep breath, and closed her eyes. "Actually, I was wondering if . . . if I could have a party this year."

The clatter stopped.

Evangeline's mother stepped back into the living room. She still wore her calm lake expression, but now it seemed as though something swirled in the depths, just out of sight—something huge. The hairs on the backs of Evangeline's arms prickled.

"A party?" her mother asked. "What kind of a party?"

"Just, you know, a regular birthday party. With cake and—"

"Of course." Her mom smiled.

"—and a few people."

The smile froze. It was still there, but in an instant it turned as cold as the snow falling outside. "People?" her mom asked. "Sweetheart, we just moved in. How could you possibly know any people to invite to a party?"

Evangeline shrugged. *Act casual.* "I met some girls on the bus. They're nice. I just thought—"

Her mom laughed and patted her on the head. "Oh, Evangeline! You don't want some random girls from the bus coming over, do you? On your special day? That wouldn't be very fun."

"It might be."

Her mom folded her arms, which meant no. "I'm sure you'll make lots of friends here," she said. "Eventually."

Evangeline rolled her eyes, not even caring how rude it was. "I *won't* make friends here. I don't make friends anywhere."

"You're being dramatic."

"No, I'm not." Evangeline raised her voice a little. "Why would anyone ever want to be friends with me? I'm always just the new girl. The girl who shows up, has nothing special about her, and leaves a few months later. I'm *invisible.*"

"I've never heard anything so selfish in my life," her mother snapped. "You know what happens to people who want to be the center of attention? They get what they wish for. And they pay for it eventually." She put a hand to her forehead.

"Fine." Evangeline got to her feet and grabbed the tub marked BLANKETS. "I'll just keep unpacking and we can go on pretending all of this is perfectly normal!"

She stomped upstairs to her mother's bedroom, dropping the tub onto the floor. She would have liked it to *crash*, but it just landed softly on the squishy carpet. Then she threw herself facedown onto her mother's bed.

It was fine for her mother to refuse to meet people and to live in these cookie-cutter houses with the shades drawn. It was just how she was. But Evangeline wanted to be more than ordinary, unnoticeable, an afterthought. She wanted a real life and real friends.

After a few minutes, Evangeline got tired of feeling sorry for herself and rolled over onto her back. With a sigh, she slid off the side of the bed, onto her feet again. She might as well put the blankets away while she was here. There always seemed to be more unpacking or packing to do.

She pulled open the big bottom drawer of her mother's bureau. It smelled like mothballs and made all the blankets smell like mothballs, too, but Evangeline dutifully unpacked the plastic tub and put everything away. She smiled at a puffy quilt with a geometric sheep design, one she'd had as a baby, and spread it over the end of the bed. There was one more blanket at the bottom of the plastic tub, a ratty old green thing spotted with mangy fuzz. But as she grasped it, she felt something hard inside. When she pulled the blanket away, there sat a little metal box.

Evangeline slid her hands underneath it and raised it to her face. She squinted at it from all angles.

It felt like secrets, but it didn't say KEEP OUT.

It wasn't locked.

With a fluttering in her chest, Evangeline settled onto the squishy carpet and lifted the metal lid of the box.

Inside, photographs of all sizes and colors shifted and rustled as she ran her fingers through them. There she was, in a tiny, cream-colored dress, sitting in the grass. There were her mother and grandparents, waving, in front of a house with peeling shutters. Evangeline thumbed through the pictures, smiling at the smiles, swallowing and blinking at the old sadnesses. Her, her mother, and sometimes her grandparents. Never other people. Never other children.

She had seen most of the pictures before. This was not really a secret box, then, just a half-forgotten one.

But there, among the old family photos, was one picture that clearly didn't belong. It flashed when Evangeline uncovered it, as though it were coated with glitter. She held it in the light.

There was a sparkling, snow-covered forest, nothing like any of the woods Evangeline had ever known. There was a frozen waterfall and, beside it, a strange tree in the middle of a cracked boulder, as though the tree itself had split the rock as it grew. She blinked—the tree was *purple*. A purple tree! And there, in the center of the picture, was a young woman holding a violin. The woman wore the most beautiful ice-blue gown Evangeline had ever seen; it sparkled like snow as the woman, captured mid-song, smiled radiantly at the person taking the photograph, whoever that was. Evangeline swore she could almost, *almost*, hear the violin's music, just at the edge of her mind. She peered at the photo, as though the woman would start dancing at any moment, her gown shimmering in the evening light.

And as she looked closer, Evangeline gasped.

The woman in the photograph was her mother. Her *mother*, who hated snow, who was the absolute last person Evangeline would expect to see outside in the wintertime wearing that stunning dress and a smile you could see from the moon. Was this what her mother used to be like? What on earth had happened to make her change so much?

"Evangeline?"

Evangeline dropped the picture as her mom came into the room. "Hi, Mom."

"I'm sorry, honey," her mother said, leaning against the doorframe. "I know it's hard on you that we have to move around so much. It's my crazy job, you know?" She shrugged. "That's real estate. Location, location, location."

"I guess." Evangeline could feel her heart beating. Could her utterly unadventurous mom really be the glamorous, gleaming person in the photo, grinning at the camera, playing some mysterious tune on the violin in the middle of a fairy forest?

"What's wrong?" Evangeline's mom took a step, then saw the photo box. "Oh, I'd forgotten about these old pictures." She picked up a Polaroid from the top of the stack. "Look at how little you were!" She sat down on the end of the bed, tilting her head at the photo. Then she looked at Evangeline. "We'll do something fun for your birthday, I promise. Okay?"

"Okay." But Evangeline couldn't contain her curiosity for a moment longer. "Mom, I—I didn't know you played the violin."

Her mother nodded. "I used to play quite a bit. But I sold the dear old thing years ago. You can't possibly remember that, can you?"

Evangeline shook her head. "No, but . . ." She picked up the snow forest photograph from the floor and held it out. "Where was this taken?"

Her mom's eyes blazed, widened. She snatched the picture from Evangeline's fingers and stared at it. Evangeline wondered if her mother would become angry—she almost *wished* for it. At least anger would be a clue, a secret, a terrible mystery. But her mother's calm lake expression didn't ripple for very long. She gave a little laugh and said, "Oh, this old picture. It's nothing. It was a Halloween party. I went as a princess. So silly." She turned the photograph over on her lap.

"But that forest!" Evangeline sat next to her on the bed. "Where is it? Tell me about it."

"Don't be ridiculous, Evangeline." Now her mother's fingers curled at the edges of the photo, gripping it. "It was a long time ago."

"But that *dress*—I've never seen you wear *anything* like—"

"Just a costume." Her mother got up. She smiled, a calm lake with ice underneath. "Let's forget it, all right? I'll go start supper." And with that, she tore the mysterious photograph to bits, shoved the pieces into her pocket, and left.

3

Evangeline dreamt of snow-blanketed forests and fairy birthday parties. She danced in a sparkling blue gown, toes crunching the icy crust, fingers tracing shapes in the air along with the sprightly song of a solitary winter violin.

She awoke to another boring Saturday in a tidy room that didn't—wouldn't ever—feel like her own. It was just the place she would stay for a while, by herself, until they moved again.

But as she blinked herself alert, she realized her toes were still chilly from that forest snow crust. How . . . ?

Then she noticed it was only her bare foot pressed up against the window, which was covered with thick morning frost. She pulled her foot back, wiggling the cold out of her toes. They had been in sunny Lakecrest for only a few days, but Evangeline was pretty sure there wasn't supposed to be thick frost on the windows in May. Or a mini-snowstorm like the one that had happened yesterday afternoon.

Evangeline shivered. *Snow.* Something wasn't right.

Her mother had always forbidden sledding and snow angels and snow forts. Evangeline didn't even own a snowsuit. And it seemed like each move took them to places with shorter and shorter winters.

She sat up and started rubbing the frost with the sleeve of her nightgown. Unlike her mother, Evangeline loved winter. Maybe that was why it seemed to follow her everywhere. But lately, the strange snow was coming more and more. It felt different, more urgent. As though it were calling her. And each time the snow came, her mother got closer to picking up and moving again.

Last time, in Greenfield, Evangeline had been given a solo in the upcoming school chorus concert. Everyone had congratulated her! Girls who had never spoken to her before were coming up to her and telling her how good her audition was. She'd been walking on air, so excited to tell her mom when she got home. Of course, a blizzard hit, the likes of which Greenfield had never seen. Snow swirled, branches grew heavy with ice and snapped like firecrackers in the woods, and Evangeline had sleepwalked out her bedroom window onto the roof and danced under the moon. They had sold the house the next week. Evangeline never spoke to any of the girls from chorus again.

She couldn't let her mother see this frosty window. She rubbed and rubbed with her sleeve, still dancing from her dream, still entranced by the violin music.

The music. Evangeline paused, frowning. It was strange, but she could swear she could still hear it. A quick, up-and-down, in-and-out melody that made her want to jump and squeal and weep and knock all the books off her shelves.

She peered over the top of the frost. Was someone actually playing a violin outside? All was sunny and calm on the street below, without a trace of winter. A woman was walking a dog. Two little kids rode bright plastic bikes at the edge of a sparkling pond in a park across the street.

Evangeline held her breath. Was it—*was it* violin music she was hearing? It was just on the edge of her mind. In the place where she felt that missing *someone*. She listened. Was the music coming from inside her own house?

It couldn't be her mother, could it?

She hurried down the stairs into the kitchen. She would give anything to see her mother playing the violin! But there was no violin and no Mom, only a note on the counter: *Grocery shopping. Back soon.*

Evangeline plopped down into a kitchen chair. She'd imagined the music. It was that photograph, that *dress*—glittering like snow, bright as the moon. She couldn't stop thinking about it. A princess costume for a Halloween party? It couldn't be. It didn't gleam cheap like a costume. It seemed heavy and deep and *real*.

The violin music looped and spiraled on the distant edge of the kitchen quiet, a jagged song she could nearly hear over the sound of her own breathing. It was as though it were trying to tell her something.

"What are you hiding, Mom?" she said aloud.

4

Evangeline poured imitation maple syrup over her golden waffles with shaking fingers, as her mother sipped a mug of mint tea and leafed through the new issue of *Arts & Culture*. She was probably reading about some new play, or an exciting art show, or an interesting museum exhibit. What was the point? They would never *go* to these things. Mom wouldn't even let Evangeline get a library card.

Tomorrow was Evangeline's birthday, and she knew her mother would try especially hard to be normal. They might even get to leave the house, who knew? As if one day a year could convince Evangeline that the way they lived somehow made sense.

The moon was full tonight. It was shimmering in the leaves of the scraggly trees outside right now. It was probably lovely. But the curtains in the kitchen were drawn. Not a finger of moonlight shone through; it had been banished just like the sunshine. Evangeline was so sick of the glow of incandescent light bulbs. The yellow light from the ceiling lamp settled in her stomach like sour milk.

She watched her mom as her eyes darted over the magazine. There was a hint of a smile at the corners of her mouth. Evangeline realized that, when her face wasn't hardened against the world, her mom was actually very beautiful. For a moment, she imagined a different life— trips to museums, sleepovers with friends, bright sunlight through clean windows, a New Year's Eve party where her mother would wear *that dress* and play "Auld Lang Syne" on the violin and everyone would clap and cheer and clink their rainbow cocktails. She could almost see all of that in her mother's face right now.

The phone rang, breaking the moment. Evangeline's stomach fluttered. Could it be Bridget and not-Bridget, the girls from the bus? Were they really interested in coming to her birthday? Maybe now she could convince Mom.

She pushed her chair back, but her mother, who was closer to the phone, stood up quickly and answered.

"Hello?" Her mom leaned against the wall with her back to Evangeline. "Who?" There was a pause. Evangeline could see her mother's shoulders stiffen. "No, I'm sorry. We're not doing anything like that . . . No, please don't. We're not interested. Goodbye." *Click*.

"Mom?" Evangeline asked as her mother turned around. "Who was that?"

Her mother's calm lake expression didn't change, but her voice faltered a little. "Who was that?"

Evangeline nodded.

Her mom shrugged. "Just a fund-raiser. The fire department."

That's a lie. It hit Evangeline like a snowball to the chest. Her mother was lying to her. That had been Bridget on the phone, or not-Bridget, she was sure of it. If only Evangeline had answered! Maybe she finally could have made friends. Now that chance was gone. Mom always got to the phone first.

Evangeline looked down at her waffles. A rush of memories flooded her brain—other kids at other schools who had reached out in small ways for a short time. Other adults who had planted seeds in her head: *Are you interested in trying out for soccer? Do you like robotics? You know, my daughter is in the chess club—is that something you think you'd enjoy?* But nothing ever came of any of it. No friends, no teams, no clubs. No chorus solo. Not even the Honor Roll Banquet she'd been invited to last year at her old school. *Ugh, that's sounds so pompous, doesn't it?* her mom had said.

Her mother had been behind all of it, she realized. Always. Sabotaging anything interesting in Evangeline's life.

She was looking at Evangeline now, serene and curious. "Are you all right, sweetie?"

Evangeline didn't answer. She wasn't all right. Something had finally broken, exploded inside her like a burst dam. The moving vans, the beige houses, the empty seats, the *secrets* . . . She'd had enough. If she sat in this dark kitchen another second, she'd start screaming.

With a clatter, Evangeline jumped out of her chair and flew up the stairs, red-faced, slamming her door. The frost on her window had grown back even thicker now and an icy layer coated her mirror, too. The room felt like a refrigerator. She sank onto the tufted stool that faced her vanity.

"She lied about the dress," she muttered. "She lied about the photograph. She's been lying to people at my schools. She *knows* something about why the snow follows me. I *know* she does." She stared at her blurry, frosty reflection. "Has my mother lied about *everything*?"

Then the frost began to move.

Evangeline squinted, sure she was imagining it. But it was unmistakable. The frost was—well, not moving, exactly, more like melting. In a small, specific spot at the center of the mirror. The spot grew, getting longer. The sight was familiar, somehow, and as Evangeline peered at it, she realized why: It reminded her of when she'd write her name in the fog on the inside of the car window. It was as though someone behind the mirror were melting a line in the frost with their finger.

As she kept watching, fascinated, the line ended, and a new one began branching off it. A moment later, she was shocked to find it looked an awful lot like the letter *y*. The invisible finger kept going, and in no time, a word was clearly visible, written in the frost:

Yes.

Evangeline clapped a hand to her mouth to avoid crying out. She put her fingers to the mirror, which was so cold it hurt to touch. Almost as soon as it formed, the *yes* began to fill in with fractals of frost again. Evangeline pulled her fingers back. "It's real, it's real," she whispered, so she wouldn't forget. So she wouldn't convince herself she had imagined it.

She kept staring at the frost-covered mirror. Something—someone—was trying to communicate with her. "What do you want?" she said, quietly at first, then louder. "What do you want?"

After Evangeline had taken four anxious breaths, the writing started again. She kept perfectly still, eyes fixed on the strange, melting tracks in the frost. The word came faster this time, the letters a little more jagged and misshapen, but in the split second between when the word was finished and when the frost started reclaiming it, Evangeline could read it perfectly:

Help.

5

Evangeline pressed her fingers to the frigid mirror. "Who are you?"

Delicate feathers of frost slowly reclaimed the mysterious word: *Help.* Soon it disappeared entirely.

"Please!" Evangeline said, her heart thumping. "Talk to me! Who are you? Are you in danger? What can I do?"

But there was no further hint of life in the frosted glass. Evangeline gripped the edges of her vanity. "No," she whispered. "Come back." Something familiar had seemed so near. A blank space filled for just a moment with someone dear and desperate. But what on earth could she do?

Downstairs, the supper dishes clinked. Evangeline thought about her mother, strange and secretive and maddeningly flat. Just a few minutes ago, Evangeline had been ready to run away, hop the next train to the farthest coast. But despite her strange ways, Mom had always been there with a hug, snack, or kind word. *Maybe* Evangeline could tell her about what she'd seen in the mirror. Maybe Mom would believe her. Maybe she'd know what to do.

With a last glance at the inscrutable mirror, Evangeline padded back out into the hallway and down the stairs. "Mom?"

Her mother was at the sink. "Are you feeling okay?" She turned to Evangeline with a look of concern. "Did you just throw up?"

Evangeline pressed her hip against the doorframe, supporting herself. "Yes. I mean, no. I didn't throw up." She hesitated, hoping for some reason that her mom would fill the silence with something. But she didn't; she just waited, leaning forward, palms on the table. Evangeline went on. "So, this really weird thing just now, in my room . . . My mirror was, um, covered with frost—"

"Frost?" Her mother tapped her fingers on the pages of her open magazine. "In May? That's ridiculous."

Evangeline hardened her voice. "Yes. It is. But it happened. It happens." She took a risk. "You *know* it happens."

Her mother crossed her arms. "There must be something wrong with the refrigerator."

The hope that had risen in Evangeline's chest started sinking. "Well, okay. Fine. But the thing is, I—saw something. In the mirror. Or—in the frost. It was moving—"

Evangeline's mother's eyes widened. She staggered backward, as though she'd been pushed by a ghost. She pointed a finger at her daughter. "Not another word. I won't hear it. You're not making sense."

"I *know* I saw something—"

"Enough!" Mom's face was stricken, as though she'd seen a terrible monster. Evangeline froze, shocked. Her mother stared at her for a moment, just as frozen. Then she grabbed her laptop from the counter and sat down at the table.

They didn't speak. Evangeline just stood, stiff, watching her mother tapping away on her computer. She didn't know what to say.

After a long moment, her mother looked up. "I'm so sorry, honey," she said in a hoarse voice. "I shouldn't have yelled. It's not your fault."

Evangeline blinked. She knew it wasn't her fault. But she wasn't sure whose fault it was.

"I don't think Lakecrest is a good place for us," her mom said. "Look at how stressed out we both are already. How are we supposed to be happy here?" She turned the laptop toward Evangeline. "Look— isn't this a beautiful little house? In a town called Springfield. Doesn't that sound like a nice place? And it was eighty degrees there today! Sounds like paradise to me."

Evangeline gaped at the screen, which showed yet another ordinary house on another ordinary street. This was a first. Her mother had never made plans to move before they'd actually finished unpacking.

The snow, the frosted mirror, the mysterious words. Evangeline knew she had to get to the bottom of this before they moved again. Because suddenly it all made sense—why her mother uprooted their lives every five minutes, why she hid behind curtains and walls.

It was because someone was looking for them. For Evangeline.

And they were *so close*.

"I'm going to bed," Evangeline said, stepping back.

Her mom kept typing, scrolling, clicking. She didn't look up. "Good night, sweetheart."

Evangeline paused in the doorway, her hand on the pale door-frame. "You can think what you want," she said quietly. "But I *know* there were words in the frost. And I know someone was writing them."

At this, her mother snapped her head in Evangeline's direction. "Wait—what did you say? *Words?* In the mirror?" Her voice shook, high and warbling, like a frightened old woman. *"Evangeline, honey,"* she whispered. *"What did the words say?"* And for the first time, Evangeline's mother couldn't hold on to her calm lake expression. Whatever giant, mysterious thing lurked just underneath had come to the surface at last. There was such a terrified glint in her eye that, for a moment, Evangeline was dumbstruck.

"Answer me!" her mother snapped, fingers gripping the edge of the table. "Evangeline, please!"

But Evangeline didn't answer. She understood. Her mother already knew about the person behind the mirror—and she had spent years protecting the secret. Evangeline fled upstairs to her room, pulling the door shut behind her and turning the lock.

Her mother came thundering up the stairs after her. "Evangeline!" She rattled the knob and pounded on the door, but couldn't get in. "Evangeline! Open this door!"

Evangeline stood with her hand on the door, breathing hard. Her mother rattled the knob again, and one more time. The door didn't budge.

Then silence. Evangeline pressed her ear to the door. She could hear her mother moving around in her room across the hall, her steps ragged thuds on the carpeting. "Mom?" she ventured.

She heard the sparkling sound of glass breaking. Evangeline drew her head back. *What on earth . . . ?* She put her ear to the door again. Her mother's footsteps thudded into the hallway. *Smash!*—more breaking glass. Then down the stairs into the living room, the kitchen. Evangeline heard one or two shatters in each room. Her skin crawled. Was her mother breaking the windows? Smashing plates?

Evangeline listened with her eyes closed. Some of the shatters were small and twinkly, some larger and shimmering. She could kind of tell where her mother was when each happened. The hallway. The mantelpiece. The bathroom. *No*, she realized. *Not windows.*

Her mother was smashing every mirror in the house.

She *did* believe Evangeline. She *knew* someone was trying to communicate with her . . .

The mirrors were the key. And Mom knew that, too.

Evangeline raced to her vanity. Her arms prickled with goose bumps from the cold that radiated from her mirror and something else that shivered inside her. What right did her mother have to keep her from whoever had written in the frost? All they had done was ask for help.

She peered into the icy mirror. It was the biggest one in the house.

"Why was my mother wearing that dress?" she cried. "Where is the snowy forest? Is that where you are? Please, I want to help you!" She needed answers *now*, before her mother came back upstairs to break down the door and smash this last mirror. Evangeline stared and stared into the frost.

Suddenly, she got the creepy feeling of someone staring back. She peered at her reflection.

The thin frost layer blurred Evangeline's edges in the glass. She squinted. Her reflection was *almost* right. But her hair seemed a little wavier, glossier. Her ears—Evangeline put a hand to her bare earlobe in surprise—the ears of her reflection wore diamonds! And there was something behind the identical eyes that just—*wasn't her*.

"Who are you?" she whispered.

Then the frost-writing started again. Evangeline watched the creation of each letter with a fierce hunger. After a minute, the reply was complete:

Your sister.

6

Evangeline's fingers started to tremble. As she looked at the words, it was as though a secret compartment in her mind sprang open. That strange cloudiness she'd been prodding and twisting her whole life suddenly clicked into clarity. *Your sister.*

She had a sister. A twin sister—the person who should have been there to sit with her on the bus, share a bag of chips, leaf through old family photographs. She had a sister who needed help, who was reaching out to her from somewhere else. And Evangeline desperately wanted to reach back.

She put her hand to the frosted mirror, tracing the clear letters. Her reflection did the same, as though it were really just a reflection, but now Evangeline knew it wasn't her own face in the glass.

Suddenly, the reflected hand turned. Evangeline felt her fingers slip through the surface of the mirror, into what felt like frigid water. She gasped. The reflected hand slid its fingers, like icicles, around her own. And started to *pull.*

"No!" Her mother's screech sliced the air as the door burst open with a *BANG*. Evangeline turned her head to see her mom dashing across the room. "Evangeline! Stop!"

But the reflected hand continued to pull. Evangeline leaned forward. Her nose touched the icy surface of the mirror, which rippled. There was something beyond, another place, a world so close she could feel the cold breeze of it on her eyelashes—

"Get back here!" Strong arms wound around Evangeline's waist, squeezing the wind out of her as they jerked her backward into her room. She landed on top of her mom with an "Oof!"

Evangeline scrabbled to her feet and lunged at the mirror.

Her mother leapt across the room. "Stand back!" she yelled. Out of the corner of her eye, Evangeline could tell she was swinging something long and black—a crowbar or a poker, swooping toward the vanity.

But Evangeline didn't stand back. She hurled herself at the mirror, pressing her face to its cold surface. It hummed like the edge of a dream she could almost remember but couldn't catch.

My sister is on the other side, she thought, closing her eyes. *She's in the place beyond this reflection and she needs my help.*

The mirror changed. It sang and burned her skin. Evangeline thought she heard the bright crash of glass shattering around her, but she focused on her sister, imagining her in an enchanted, snow-covered forest, playing their mother's violin.

And just as she heard the first notes of the song, though she couldn't tell if they came from the room behind her or the inside of her own brain or somewhere else entirely, she melted headfirst into the surface of the mirror.

7

Evangeline fell through the frost-covered mirror into cold silver space. Her stomach lurched and looped. *Up* and *down* and *sideways* kept changing places. Finally, she hit the ground, palms first, with a *smack*.

"Oof!" She rolled onto her back. It was a bright, chilly day. Snatches of conversations, cries, and laughter swirled around her in the crisp air. The brilliant blue sky above her was framed by the tops of slanted gingerbread houses, and the flagstones beneath her vibrated with the *thump-thump-thump* of heavy animal feet.

I'm here! she thought, immediately followed by, *But where am I?*

Evangeline sat up. She was in what must be a town square; she recognized the feel of it from fairy tales. In fact, the whole place felt like a fairy tale. Buildings with pitched roofs decorated like icing on cakes leaned together over striped market stalls crowded with shoppers and idlers dressed in thick, bright cloth.

The ground here was muddy and half-frozen, icicles hung from gutters, and a snowy wind billowed through Evangeline's handmade sweater, a birthday gift from her grandmother. It had come in the mail last week, as white as snow and as soft as a kitten. On the hem, Evangeline had pinned a bright plastic button she'd found in the schoolyard. It said JELLY BEAN HUGS and had a picture of two jelly beans smiling and hugging. Evangeline hugged herself in the cold. She didn't even have shoes on.

Wait—if it was morning, that must mean it was now her birthday. She was twelve. And so was her twin sister, wherever she was. Did her sister have birthday parties here in this fairy-tale land, with cake and friends?

"Out of the way!" a voice boomed as a rickety wagon nearly ran Evangeline over.

"Oh! Sorry!" she called after it, astonished by the great, hairy creatures that pulled the wagon along—they looked like white bears with wide cows' heads and tufted lions' tails.

I'm definitely not in Lakecrest anymore, she thought. *Or was it Crestlake?*

People and carts flowed around her as she stared, leaving the scents of bread, flowers, and the strange, fuzzy bear-cows in their wakes. There was no sign of her sister anywhere.

"Get up, get up!" a piercing voice barked above the rest of the din. "Stop lying in the street, you half-wit!"

Evangeline got to her feet and looked around. Everyone was busy going here and there, talking to friends, browsing the market for teapots and woolly socks and dead fish. Nobody was paying her any attention, except—

She noticed a pair of golden eyes at the edge of the street, staring. At her.

The eyes flashed in and out of sight as people passed by, but the gaze remained steady. Evangeline struggled to make out the shape of the gazer in the crowd—white, purple, and small. It was a *fox*. A white fox! What were they called? *Arctic fox*, she remembered, a snow fox built for harsh winters. He was sitting perfectly still, his long bushy tail curled around his front paws and a luxurious purple-and-gold cape draped across his back.

Had—had this fox spoken to her? Evangeline glanced left and right. People passed her by without a second glance, like the whole town square was a schoolyard at recess and she didn't know any of the other kids. Except for this staring fox. His wide, golden-eyed gaze never wavered. And he almost seemed . . . annoyed?

Then, though she told herself she *must* be imagining it, the fox jerked his nose, twice, in a gesture that clearly said, *Come here.*

Evangeline tilted her head in disbelief.

The fox blinked slowly. He was definitely annoyed. He gestured with his paw. Pointing at her!

Evangeline jutted a thumb at her chest. "Me?"

The fox rolled his eyes and nodded. Now Evangeline was sure she was imagining it. Maybe if you didn't use your imagination enough, it started messing with you. But the snow fox was still watching her with golden eyes.

He wagged his head again, more insistent. *Come here!*

Evangeline gave a shudder, trying to shake reality back into her brain. *A white fox is clearly gesturing for me to come speak to him,* she thought. *And it's not even the weirdest thing that's happened to me this weekend.*

But she made her way through the throng to the edge of the flag-stoned street until she was looking down at the strange little animal.

"Did you . . . did you—" she began.

"Well. All I can say is it's *about time,*" the fox said, rather snippily. "Now, come on." He started trotting away down the sidewalk, his cape billowing. Evangeline followed.

"I—what?" she asked. "Look, I was wondering if you could help—"

"Zzzzzp!" The fox turned around and made a zipping gesture.

"But—"

"*Zip. It.*"

Evangeline shut her mouth. He was kind of a rude little fox.

"Tell it to the Lord High Keeper." The fox paused in the shelter of a grand, arched doorway. He shook his head. "I cannot *imagine* the paperwork your little escapade is going to cause me, thank you very much." He grasped a thin rope that hung from above the door with his teeth and pulled. With a venerable creak, the heavy door swung open. "Come on, we'll soon get you sorted."

"I—oh. Good." Evangeline had no idea what was going on, but this fox seemed to know what he was doing. Maybe he could help her find her sister.

The arched door opened onto an echoey room with a gold-and-white tiled floor. The ceiling stretched up into four high peaks supported by marble pillars. Bookshelves and narrow doors lined the walls. People bustled here and there, carrying files and ornate cylinders or leaning against the wall sipping from mugs. The people were all shapes and sizes, some with long, pointed ears, clouds of vibrant hair, or large, clawed feet with knees that seemed to be pointing the wrong way. Evangeline stared, trying to take it all in.

The fox trotted over to a polished counter and hopped up onto a stool so he could speak to the woman behind it. She had tiny red eyes and was busy stamping papers with a heavy rubber stamp. Evangeline sauntered over to them.

"Sir Paw-on-Stone, Knight of the Winter Kingdom, Fourth Keeper of the Crystal Gate," the fox said haughtily as the woman wrote something with a long, skinny blue pen. "Turning in."

"Offense?" the woman asked in a voice as exciting as soggy cardboard.

"Have you eyes, woman?" The fox gestured to Evangeline, and the red-eyed woman looked up.

Her expression turned from sour milk to shock. She looked from Evangeline to the fox and back again. "Wait here!" The woman flashed a meaningful look over Evangeline's shoulder and snapped her fingers.

Evangeline turned to see two large men with shiny, pointed helmets taking a step closer as the woman hurried away across the floor.

"What's going on?" Evangeline asked. "Look, Mr. Fox, I need your help. I've got to find my sis—"

The cape-wearing fox gave her a stern look. "Sir *Paw*-on-*Stone*."

"Sorry." Evangeline stepped away from the pointed helmets and appealed to Sir Paw-on-Stone. "My mom smashed all the mirrors, but I went through the last one before she got to it—"

The fox put a paw on her hand to shush her. "This whole amnesia thing, or whatever you're doing, is not going to help. Trust me. Just tell the truth and all will be forgiven, Your—"

"What are you talking about?" Evangeline interrupted. "I am telling the truth!" She heard the clop of boots behind her taking a cautious step in her direction. The pointy-helmet guards apparently didn't like her outburst.

Sir Paw-on-Stone tilted his head. "Oh, *really*?" he said sarcastically. "What was it again, you came through a *mirror*? A mirror portal. Into Rime Village. And I suppose you came from *Terra*, is that it?"

"Terra?" Evangeline asked. "You—you mean Earth? Of course I'm from Earth!"

The fox huffed. "Preposterous! Your lies are only getting worse as you get older." He cleared his throat. "Happy birthday, by the way."

"I—thank you," Evangeline said, wondering how he knew. "But I told you, I'm here to find my sister. So much has happened. There was a photograph of my mom in a blue dress playing the violin by a purple tree—"

"Poppycock!" the fox yipped. "Playing *one of those* is strictly forbidden, as you well know. And as for the purple tree, well, that's simply the biggest lie you've ever told me, which is quite an accomplishment!"

Playing a violin is forbidden? Evangeline thought. *What is the matter with this place?* But she had bigger concerns. "I need your help," she pleaded. "I think my sister's in trouble! I really am from Terra. Look, I . . ." Did she have any proof? Something from Earth, that clearly didn't belong in Rime Village, the Winter Kingdom, whatever this place was? Her mind raced. Her corduroys didn't look so different from some of the other pants she could see here, her sweater was handmade, she didn't wear contact lenses, she had no cell phone . . .

"Here!" She fumbled with the hem of her sweater. "Here, look!" And she held out her JELLY BEAN HUGS button.

The fox frowned at the button, then frowned at Evangeline. He took the button in his paw and studied it. "Is this some kind of magic spell?"

"Magic?" Evangeline gave him a puzzled look. "No. It's just a button. You pin it on. See, like this." She slid the pin through the gold edging of the fox's purple cape and attached it. "It's jelly beans. They're an Ear—a Terra candy. You don't have jelly beans here, right? That's proof."

The fox looked skeptical. "We have both jelly and beans, thank you very much." He peered at the pin, swiveling his eyes downward and puffing out his chest. "Although they do not grin and hug each other."

"Well, Earth jelly beans don't, either," Evangeline said, her great idea feeling less and less great by the moment. "These are just drawn that way. They're all happy and hugging because . . . I don't really know." She looked down. "It's kind of stupid, I guess. I picked it up because it was colorful. Like a magpie."

The fox continued to stare at the button. He sniffed it and recoiled. Then a strange expression came over his face. "How did you get this curious brooch? Tell the truth. Think carefully."

"How?" Evangeline tried to keep her voice low, but it cracked. "I found it on the ground in the schoolyard on Terra, where I've lived my whole life. I was born there!"

Sir Paw-on-Stone narrowed his golden eyes. "You were most certainly *not* born there. Do you think I'm a fool? I'm a Keeper of the Crystal Gate! Look, you've turned yourself in at last, and King Vair may show you leniency because of that. Why do you insist on this ridiculous story?"

Evangeline felt her face getting hot. She took a deep breath. "Turn myself in? King *who*? *What?*"

The pointy-helmet guards were right behind her now, the clomp of their boots echoing off the marble pillars.

"I haven't done anything wrong!" Evangeline cried. "I'm just looking for my sister, I promise! I saw her through my vanity. I tried to go with her, but my mom tried to stop me, and then she broke all our mirrors, and—"

Their conversation was halted by the approach of thudding footsteps that boomed and squeaked like thick ice. The room shuddered.

Evangeline looked up. Striding toward them was the most remarkable, frightening person she'd ever laid eyes on. He was as tall as two of her put together, and his shoulders, covered by a neat black coat that nearly touched the floor, were as wide as a dresser. He wore a puffy black velvet hat with a fan of feathers sticking up on the side, and black leather gloves. But the most striking thing about him was his grayish-white skin, which was bright and hard, as though it had been chiseled from a glacier. In fact, if Evangeline didn't know better, she'd think the man himself had been carved out of ice.

All chatter and bustle in the place died as the enormous ice man crossed the floor. People who happened to be standing near doorways ducked out of sight. Others slipped behind bookcases. Those caught out in the open stood very straight and folded their hands behind their backs.

The ice man was headed right for Evangeline. She took a few backward steps toward the front door, but felt a heavy hand on her shoulder. The two pointy-helmet guards were blocking her path.

The ice man stopped in front of Evangeline and stared at her with hard, shiny eyes like blue marbles. The big room, which had been noisy and alive only moments before, was utterly silent, as though even the marble pillars were holding their breath.

"Here she is," said a flat voice, and Evangeline saw the red-eyed woman standing behind the ice man.

"She has come willingly, Lord High Keeper," the white fox said.

"I see," the ice man—the Lord High Keeper—rumbled, vibrating the tiles on the floor. It was the voice a mountain would have if mountains could talk. He continued to stare at Evangeline, f~ she looked back into his blue-marble eyes, waiting—for w

After a long moment, the gray-white lips slowly curved into a smile. Evangeline started to breathe again as relief washed over her. She smiled back.

"Finally," the Lord High Keeper said in that low, rumbling voice.

"Look," Evangeline said, "this is all a mistake. I'm not turning myself in for anything. I—" She was cut off by a poke in the back as the guards crowded even closer. She could smell their breath, like stale bread.

The enormous man's smile broadened, revealing four rows of shining, sharp icicle teeth. Suddenly, Evangeline didn't feel quite so relieved anymore.

"Call off the hunt, gentlemen!" the Lord High Keeper bellowed like a mountain exploding. "We've caught her at last."

"Wait!" Evangeline cried. "This is wrong! I'm not—" But the Lord High Keeper clapped his massive hands together, stifling her words. His whole body flashed, like the glare of sunlight on a frozen lake. A circular patch in the air in front of him shimmered into a haze. It looked to Evangeline like some kind of doorway, made from sparkling, translucent grease. Where it led was anyone's guess.

"Hey!" Evangeline yelped as the great ice man thrust an arm around her waist and picked her up like an old duffel bag. But he didn't reply. He just strode through the greasy portal.

8

There was a rush of wind and then it was over. Evangeline was *there*, and now she was *here*. It wasn't at all like pressing herself through the mirror from Earth into the Winter Kingdom. The Lord High Keeper's portal felt cruder than the mirror passageway in Evangeline's room, like the difference between staggering through rough wooden saloon doors and sliding into a pool of liquid silver.

Once they were through, the Lord High Keeper set Evangeline on her feet again with a *thud*. She didn't care where she was—her first instinct was to run. But once she caught sight of her surroundings, she stopped.

The first things she saw were two gleaming rows of soldiers at attention. They wore matching blue armor and held spear-like weapons with ends like long, clawed axes. Their helmets hid any hint of facial expressions, except for the rectangular cutouts that revealed a glimpse of each soldier's triple-eye set in smooth, greenish skin.

The rows of soldiers formed a pathway to a wide set of marble steps, which led to a gigantic golden door; one of those doors that is so large and heavy, it has smaller doors cut into it that people can actually use. Evangeline's gaze traveled to the top of the door, then up, up, and *up* the face of a great, feathery castle. The castle's walls were made from white stone that reminded her of opals, the way whispers of color seemed to flicker across the surface. Everything shone in the winter sun. Evangeline stood and squinted at the glare.

"King Vair will be very interested in what you have been up to," the Lord High Keeper rumbled darkly. He prodded Evangeline in the back and she started walking. She had no other choice. In truth, there was a small part of her that yearned to see what was beyond that huge golden palace door. The soldiers in their shiny blue armor were still and silent as Evangeline and the Lord High Keeper passed between their two straight rows.

King Vair. Was Evangeline to meet the king of this strange country? Everyone here seemed to think Evangeline was someone else— her sister, of course, who was some kind of fugitive. Was that why she had asked Evangeline for help? But what could her sister have done to attract the attention of the king himself? It must have been very bad. Evangeline's stomach did a nauseous little flip.

She had to hop-walk to keep up with the Lord High Keeper in his long black coat as he strode heavily up the marble steps. On the other side of the palace door, she was surprised to find a beautiful garden, full of strange, pale flowers and splashing fountains. A page boy with far too many feathery fingers and wide, wet eyes like a fish emerged. The Lord High Keeper paused to speak to him.

Evangeline marveled at the garden. Intricate ice sculptures decorated the grounds, like fancy party centerpieces in Mom's art magazines. They were all sculptures of people, though some looked like peasants and some like aristocrats. They were tall and short, both human-looking and otherworldly, like the inhabitants of Rime Village—except for one sculpture that was just a pair of boots surrounded by a puddle of clear water. At the base of each sculpture was a white card. TWO DAYS, one of the cards read. ONE WEEK, read another. And below a carving of a hunched old man with an ice violin under one arm, the white card said, FOREVER. Evangeline got chills looking at it, although she didn't know why. In truth, the longer she admired the ice sculptures, the more she found she didn't actually like them. There was something sad about the way they stood slightly dripping in the winter sunshine.

In the center of the garden was a calm pond. Its gray lily pads and white flowers caught Evangeline's attention, and as the Lord High Keeper continued to rumble at the poor page boy, she drifted over.

Evangeline gazed at her reflection in the still water. If she tilted her head just so and crossed her eyes a tiny bit, she could see something moving behind the image of her face. A fish? No. The movement wasn't *in* the pond; it was beyond it. In the place beyond her reflection. She peered into the water, trying to make it out . . .

A girl! Could it be her sister? Evangeline kept staring. The girl wore a long black cloak. She was creeping, crouching, running in little spurts. Every once in a while, she would look back over her shoulder with a frightened expression. Evangeline's heart jumped into her throat. The girl looked just like her. It *was* her sister. It had to be.

Suddenly, the girl stopped. Her eyes swiveled, her brows knotted. She seemed to be staring straight at Evangeline!

Evangeline's breath caught. Her sister's mouth opened. Her lips formed a word: *Evangeline?*

"Yes," Evangeline whispered. "Yes! It's me!"

Her sister's eyes grew wide, even more fearful. She shook her head. "No. No!" Evangeline could hear her words now, faintly.

Then the girl in the cloak glanced over her shoulder again, turning quickly back to Evangeline. She spoke only three more words, urgently, staring into Evangeline's eyes from across this strange space between places. The sound was fuzzy, swirling, but the words were unmistakable: "Don't trust Father!"

Then everything around Evangeline's sister began to glow with a dazzling violet light. And as it washed over the landscape, she disappeared.

Evangeline dropped to her knees and touched her forehead to the water. The pond was cool and smelled like fish and green things. "Come back," she whispered.

Her insides twisted. *Don't trust Father.*

She'd never known her father. Their father. Her mother had told her he wasn't a very nice man. "And I wasn't his greatest love," Mom had said, with such a pained expression that she had never asked again. Evangeline didn't miss him. He'd never felt like part of her life, just a distant shape in the fog of a past she had no connection to. Was he here, now, in the Winter Kingdom? Maybe *he* was what her sister had been trying to escape from when she disappeared in that flash of violet light.

Evangeline had to find out—but who in all of the Winter Kingdom could help her? *Nobody*, she realized. If her sister had reached across worlds for help, maybe Evangeline was her only hope.

"Get up!" the Lord High Keeper barked. Evangeline got to her feet and went over to him.

"I will inform His Majesty at once, Your Highness," the page boy said in a voice like tiny bubbles.

Your Highness, Evangeline thought. Could the Lord High Keeper, this frightening ice man, be some kind of royalty? Then, with a shock, she noticed the page boy was looking at *her*. He flashed Evangeline a tiny smile. "It is so good to see you home safe, Princess Desdemona," he said warmly before pattering away.

Evangeline's eyes widened. She remembered the diamonds, as big as almonds, that dripped from the ears of the girl in the mirror. But if her sister was royalty—a princess!—did that mean Evangeline was also . . .

Princess Evangeline?

For a moment, she was stunned. But then she regained herself. *No,* she thought. *You are Evangeline Reynolds, from Earth, and you're just here to help your sister. It doesn't matter what she is in this world. There's nothing "princess" about you in any way.*

At the end of the garden, a giant staircase curved away up to a tall, lacy door. Its railings were like an ocean wave that had frozen just as it crashed on the shore, and as Evangeline followed the Lord High Keeper up, she ran her fingers along the remarkable railing. It was chilly and a little electric to the touch, not like ice at all, but like liquid water being held against its will.

The Lord High Keeper led Evangeline down a carpeted hallway, which glowed yellow in the light of standing brass candelabras. She did her best not to be distracted by the suits of armor, the dark portraits, and the fat vases of pale flowers. She was supposed to be her sister, Princess Desdemona, and this was the princess's home.

Desdemona going gaga over the stuff in the palace hallway would be like Evangeline back on Earth stopping to appreciate the toaster.

They came to a set of doors made of varnished white wood and carved to look like swans. *This is her room*, Evangeline thought.

"Wait in your suite," the Lord High Keeper rumbled.

Suite. That didn't sound too bad. Evangeline couldn't help leaning forward as the Lord High Keeper turned a silver key in the lock. When he pushed open one of the swan doors, she all but ran inside.

Then the door closed and she heard the *click* of a key turning.

"Locked in!" Evangeline said. She whirled around and grasped the curving door handle, rattling it and pressing on the sturdy white wood with her shoulder. The swan doors didn't budge. After a minute, she gave up.

"Maybe there's some clue in here," she muttered. "Some message she left." She couldn't get the image of her sister's frightened face out of her mind. Princess Desdemona was in danger; Evangeline was sure of it. Wherever she had gone, and for whatever reason, she had to track her down.

She leaned against the door, taking in her sister's room. "Oh!" she cried, without even meaning to. It was an *oh* bursting with opposites. *Oh*, the space!—a domed ceiling that spread like the sky itself, marble pillars like trees, a canopy bed that would fit a napping elephant.

Oh, the colors, textures, scents!—shining blue and purple silks, diamonds glinting from drawer pulls, thick, feathery rugs, and minty white candles reflecting off polished silver sconces. And *oh, oh*, the sinking, twisty feeling that washed over Evangeline as she beheld it all. This was the place where Desdemona had slept and dressed and done homework—if princesses even *had* homework—while Evangeline was shuffled from boring beige house to boring beige house. Could this have been her life? Could she have grown up here, with Desdemona, two princesses of the Winter Kingdom? Why would Mom take her away from all this luxury and beauty? Why did Desdemona get to be a princess, while Evangeline was just a *nobody*?

Being somebody apparently isn't working out too well for your sister right now, Evangeline told herself. Hadn't her mother said something like that? She couldn't remember.

Evangeline padded across the room to find a wide closet just where she thought it would be. Inside hung sparkling dresses of every color. None of them were quite as beautiful as the ice-blue gown in Mom's photograph, but they were definitely several cuts above anything Evangeline had ever owned. She pushed dress after dress aside—wispy lace, embroidered silk, silver like a waterfall. But nothing in the closet hinted at where the princess might have gone.

The bedroom was closed off by a large painted screen, and there was a turquoise door that led to a bathroom so fancy the tub had stairs leading up to it. Evangeline riffled through drawers, pulled back curtains, and peeked under silver settees. She opened jewelry boxes and pulled the crystal stoppers from perfume bottles. She imagined her sister choosing a jeweled necklace for the day and spraying a cloud of floral scent over her gown. Would she and Evangeline have dressed alike?

Finally, Evangeline seated herself on a stool tufted with aquamarine satin and pulled open a polished desk drawer. Inside were papers of all sorts and sizes, gilded and intricately cut. Evangeline slid a few letters from their envelopes; nothing too interesting. *Thank you for attending* such and such, *the weather remains fine here in* wherever, and so on and so on. Nobody wrote letters to Evangeline, especially not in fancy envelopes with wax seals on them. She dropped them onto the desk and reached deeper into the drawer, pulling out a single sheet of paper that had been shoved almost all the way to the back.

The paper was covered with a strange collection of notes and scribbles that Evangeline couldn't make heads or tails of. One column was a list of what seemed to be strange names: Sir Quilted Wing, Lady Six Green Trees, Madam Walks-Through-Walls, Sir Paw-on-Stone . . . There were twelve names altogether. Eight of them had been crossed out for some reason. Another list contained titles like *The Red Tunnels*, *Bright Mine*, *Overset Gorge Mine*, and others, and next to each one was a series of numbers. "Bright Mine" had been circled, along with its curious tally: *57, 72, 108, 213.* Evangeline ran her fingers along the list. Why was her sister keeping track of these mines? What did the figures mean—something being dug there? The workers? Bright Mine was the only place where the numbers kept increasing. Pieces of thoughts were jotted next to the list, all questions: *Crystal? Prisoners? Aranae?* Then a word written more forcefully and underlined twice: *Rootball??*

Even though Evangeline had no idea what the notes meant, one thing was clear. Her sister had been trying to piece something together. She'd been investigating.

"Is this why you ran away?" Evangeline murmured.

She slid her hand back into the recesses of the desk, her fingers finding one last object—something smooth. If she hadn't been in the Winter Kingdom, she would have thought it was a photograph.

Evangeline grasped the paper with her fingertips and pulled it out from the back of the drawer. It *was* a photograph! She stared at it, her heart fluttering. A beautiful, snowy forest—the Winter Kingdom, she now knew. And a woman with a violin. It was Evangeline's mother. She looked a little sadder in this image, and wasn't playing the violin. Instead, she was holding it at her side. Behind her was the same cracked boulder and purple tree as in the photograph on Earth.

Purple tree. Evangeline peered at the tree in the background. It seemed to be glowing, violet light gleaming from its bark and leaves and making violet shadows on the white snow.

It looked just like the light she had seen surrounding her sister when she disappeared.

A sharp knock at the door startled her. "Princess Desdemona!" came the booming voice of the Lord High Keeper.

Evangeline tossed the photo onto the desk and strode across the room. *Princess,* she thought, trying to keep her posture regal and her chin high. For now, she had to pretend. Because something told her whatever it was her sister had learned about the people and places in her secret, scribbled notes had put her in very real danger.

The cavernous blue room was lined with windows that cast bright slices of white on the polished stone floor, as though a giant's sword had pierced the walls, leaving a series of two-story-tall cuts.

This was unmistakably the throne room. *But why does it have to be so large?* Evangeline wondered. After all, the only furniture it needed to house was a single chair. Okay, that chair was enormous, stretching away toward the vaulted ceiling like an explosion of sapphires, but still—it was *one chair*. Why did the throne room need to be so vast and echoey? Was it just to make people nervous?

If so, it was working. Evangeline ran her damp palms along the sides of her corduroys. Her bare feet squeaked on the polished floor as the Lord High Keeper herded her farther into the room. When they reached the center, he stopped and stood as still as the strange ice statues in the garden. Evangeline noticed the page boy they had met earlier in the garden standing stiffly next to the sapphire throne.

After a moment, a door on the other side of the room opened. A round little man with thinning, watery hair appeared. He was dressed in thick velvet and masses of gold and jewels. A golden mask, molded into a long beak, like a heron's, stretched across the middle of his face, leaving his mouth and haughty eyes uncovered.

King Vair, Evangeline thought. Then, with a jolt—*is* he *my father?* She'd been so wrapped up in thoughts of her new sister . . . of course a princess's father would be a king. How could she have been so clueless? Her lungs tightened. She wondered if she would fall over then and there.

As the man approached, she searched for something of herself in his scowling, flushed appearance. He waddled purposefully across the blue floor toward Evangeline and the Lord High Keeper, the page boy bowing his head as he passed. The king grunted and huffed under the weight of his trappings. By the time he reached Evangeline, he was quite out of breath, panting wetly through his mouth, as the heron mask covered his nose completely.

"I—" she began, not knowing what to say.

"Silence," came a commanding voice, making her jump. Evangeline turned to see another man. He entered the room through a larger doorway behind her, steady and straight as a pin, scowling and flanked by four golden-armored guards whose helmets sported long plumes of every color. This man was very tall and very thin and wore a long white leather coat with steel buttons. His eyes were a fierce, silvery gray, and everything about him seemed long and pointed, from his fingers to his ears. Black hair like glass fell to his shoulders, and on his head he wore a thin steel circlet. Around his neck hung a heavy pendant set with a glittering blue sapphire that seemed to wear rainbows under its skin.

Evangeline gasped as she met the man's gaze. It was the same feeling she'd had when she saw the ice-blue ball gown in her mother's photograph. This man was not a Halloween costume. He was *real*. And he was terrifying.

"Father," Evangeline whispered.

9

"Don't 'Father' me," King Vair said coldly, in a voice like the bottom of the sea.

For a split second, Evangeline's heart jumped into her throat—the king must know she wasn't really the princess. But he didn't seem suspicious. He just brushed by her, followed by his golden-armored bodyguards, and sat, as upright as a piano teacher, on the tall sapphire throne.

"What news, Lord Gilded Fingers?" the king said to the round man in the heron beak mask. "Good or ill?"

"Grave news, Your Majesty," the man said, bowing. "Grave, grave news. We have been unable to contact Sir Quilted Wing, and fear his ship was lost."

King Vair closed his eyes and sighed. "A terrible tragedy." He pointed a long finger at the heron-beaked man. "We *must* get to the bottom of this. The Keepers are *vital* to the security of the Winter Kingdom." He spoke in a low, bristling voice. "Do not rest, Lord Gilded Fingers. Do not rest. Our people come first."

"Yes, Your Majesty." The masked man bowed deeply and scurried away.

Now the king turned his gaze to Evangeline, staring at her with steely eyes and drumming his long fingers on the arm of the sapphire throne. She thought she might collapse into a heap.

But then she remembered *Alice in Wonderland*. Third grade. North Pond Elementary School Drama Club. Oh, her mother would never have let her be *in* the drama club. She wouldn't even let Evangeline go to the performance. But the club did their dress rehearsal during the school day, in front of their classmates, so Evangeline had gotten to see the play after all. And what she remembered, right now, was the Queen of Hearts. The Queen of Hearts hadn't been a real queen. She had been a girl named Lizzie who liked green beans and snorted when she laughed. But during the performance of *Alice in Wonderland*, Lizzie had stood up very straight, put her hands on her hips, and said in the most commanding voice, "Off with her head!" She had been a queen in that moment.

Evangeline stood up very straight, hiding her trembling hands behind her back. "Hello, Your Majesty."

King Vair didn't bellow like the Lord High Keeper. He was as smooth as polished stone. But his eyes burned with cloud-dark fire. "*Where* have you *been*?"

"Uh . . . Rime Village," Evangeline said, remembering the name of the fairy-tale town she'd tumbled into through the mirror.

The king crossed his arms. His white leather elbows stuck out sharp like the points of a star. "Is that where you got those peasant clothes?" he said, the word *peasant* all spit and hiss.

Evangeline used her best Queen of Hearts voice. "Yes. I wanted to fit in."

"That is hardly possible," the king said.

"Thank you."

It seemed to Evangeline that, for just a flash, King Vair looked impressed. He turned to the great ice man. "Lord High Keeper, thank you for returning my daughter to me."

The Lord High Keeper bowed. Evangeline began to relax. A princess—her! It wasn't true, of course, but she was playing the part pretty well. Her voice had never been so confident. Her posture had never been so good.

"He was quite rude, actually," she said, raising her nose and giving the Lord High Keeper a snobby look. His blue-marble eyes narrowed, but he didn't say anything.

King Vair gave a dry laugh. Then he leaned forward. "I am relieved you are safe, Princess Desdemona. Let's put this behind us, shall we?"

Evangeline nodded. It was bizarre, talking to this stranger who was her father. But for all his sharply pointed appearance, he seemed to be glad she—Desdemona—had returned unharmed. She felt her shoulders starting to relax.

King Vair steepled his long fingers. "Now, tell me: When can I expect your sister to join us? I'm eager for our long-overdue family reunion."

Evangeline gave a start. "My—sister?" The king meant *her*—Evangeline. He wanted her here? Why had Mom kept all of this a secret?

She thought she saw a flicker in the king's eyes. He inhaled. "Surely you wouldn't have returned to the palace if you were *still* unwilling to help me? Surely not, Desdemona?" His voice softened. "All I want is for us to be a family again."

Evangeline didn't know what to say to him. She had a family—her mother. And Princess Desdemona, that missing *someone* who had always haunted her. But this man? This stranger whose gray eyes narrowed in the harsh light? King Vair had wanted to bring Evangeline to the Winter Kingdom. And Princess Desdemona had refused to help him. The thought hurt. Had Desdemona not wanted to see her?

Her sister's words thrummed in her ears: *Don't trust Father.* Evangeline gulped. It felt like she was suddenly in the middle of a life-or-death game and she didn't know the rules.

She had to gain the upper hand somehow. Then she remembered Desdemona's notes. Summoning as much bravery as she could, she said, "I know about Bright Mine."

King Vair blinked. Then he smiled. "Of course you do. You've always been so observant. Maddeningly so."

Evangeline, of course, didn't know anything at all about Bright Mine, except that Desdemona had been keeping track of *something* going on there. But if her sister was observant, she could be, too. She studied the king's face. His smile hid an uncertainty. It was a look Mom had sometimes, when she seemed just about to reveal something important. She never did, but Evangeline recognized the expression anyway.

Then the king nodded and gestured, both hands palm-up. "Why hide it from my own daughter any longer? You're right. You've been right all along. For twelve years, the miners have tunneled, not for crystal, but toward the rootball itself."

She thought she heard a sharp inhalation, as though someone, or maybe more than one person, had been shocked by the king's words. Evangeline's eyes darted around the vast blue room. The page boy's fish eyes were wide, but he stood still as stone. The golden-armored guards' expressions were hidden behind their helmets. The Lord High Keeper's face was chiseled nothingness.

Rootball. That word had been underlined in Desdemona's notes. What did it mean?

"The—the rootball," Evangeline said, trying to keep her voice even.

King Vair stood, a fierce excitement overpowering him. "We are so close, Desdemona! I suspect we will strike it within the next few days. Then I will unlock the secret of the rootball stone—immortality!"

Immortality! What is he talking about? Evangeline wondered. This all seemed so ridiculous.

The king calmed down. "It is my greatest wish to share that moment with my family." He lowered himself once again onto the sapphire throne. "The truth is, I need you there. What good is immortality without family to share it with? So tell me—make my heart happy, my dear—will you help us reunite with your poor lost sister?"

Evangeline tried to stay in character. *Be a princess, not a nervous nobody. Stay in control.* It all started to make sense. King Vair had been looking for her, maybe all her life. Was that why they moved so much? And now he thought Desdemona could find her, succeed where he had failed. Maybe she had been feeling Evangeline's presence more and more, the way Evangeline had felt hers.

What would the king do if he knew it wasn't the princess who stood before him now, but his long-lost Earth daughter? Evangeline didn't like the way his eyes glinted when he talked about immortality, and this rootball stone. There was something vicious about him. Every atom in her body told her she had to keep her secret.

She flashed what she hoped was a comfortable smile. "Perhaps I will help you."

"Ah," King Vair said. He paused, his thin mouth turning down in a slight frown. *"Perhaps."*

The king got to his feet and took two graceful steps down from the polished blue dais that held the sapphire throne. Then he turned to the fish-eyed page boy, who stood at attention nearby. "You," he said, pointing. The page boy's eyes grew fearful. "Tell me—what do you think of 'perhaps'?"

The page boy's mouth opened. His gaze jerked frantically from the king to the princess and back again. Evangeline's chest fluttered just a little. What did her father mean?

"I . . . uh . . . ," the page boy floundered.

"I can wait." The king's voice was soft, but something about it shuddered the sapphires in their delicate settings. "What do you think of 'perhaps,' boy?"

The page boy was shaking so hard, Evangeline feared his legs would give way. "Father—" she started.

"No thoughts, my lad?" King Vair pointed a clawed finger at the terrified servant. "Why don't you think about it and present me with an answer later? Let's say—a week."

Then two things happened at once. The page boy fell to his knees, shouting, "Please, n—!" And a jet of white-blue light, or crystal, or something in between, shot from the end of the king's long finger and hit him square in the chest.

Evangeline gasped. There was the page boy, kneeling, a stricken look on his face, his mouth open in protest. But now he was made entirely of ice.

The king turned to one of the golden-armored guards. He waved a hand carelessly toward the frozen servant. "Have it put in the garden with the others."

The guard bowed. "At once, Your Majesty."

Evangeline was just as frozen as the page boy. *A week*, the king had said. That was what the little white cards meant. Those sculptures were real people, and the cards were the length of their sentences—doomed to sit, frozen and alone, until he turned them back again. *If* he turned them back again. She thought of the card that said FOREVER. Then she remembered the horrible statue that was simply a pair of ice boots in the middle of a puddle. *Whoever that was will never be turned back again*, she realized with a lurch in her stomach. And the king had done this to them all. He was a tyrant!

How could you? she wanted to say to him, but the words turned to less-than-whispers in her throat. She didn't feel in the least like a princess anymore, or even a pretend Queen of Hearts. As the king turned his attention back to her, as he caught her in a storm-cloud gaze, she was afraid.

"Well, Princess Desdemona," King Vair said. His quiet words filled the vast throne room. "I don't care for 'perhaps.' I don't care for it at all. It sounds like a negotiation. And I do not negotiate. I command." He ascended the dais and seated himself once again on the sapphire throne. Then his expression turned to one of sadness. "You caused me great pain when you ran away, my dear," he said, and Evangeline thought, *Lies*. The king sighed. "How ever shall I keep you safe now? You've proven to me that you simply can't be trusted."

There was a barely audible rumble from the direction of the huge Lord High Keeper. It might have been a laugh.

"Me, untrustworthy?" Evangeline said. "At least I don't turn people to ice!" She couldn't imagine anyone trusting this cruel, cold shadow of a king.

King Vair leaned forward. "When I say I need you and your sister to share my moment of triumph when I awaken the rootball stone—I do mean it, my dear. But since you *persist* in disobeying me, I have no choice but to send you to Bright Mine with the criminals. It's the only way I can protect you, Desdemona. No one ever escapes from Bright Mine." He jerked his head, his voice hardening. "Lord High Keeper. It's the mine for the princess. And"—the king frowned, as though pained by what he must say next—"a mortal band. To keep her out of trouble."

"A what? I—" Evangeline started.

"I'm sorry, Princess," the king said. "You force my hand." He ran two long fingers down the glittering blue pendant that hung over his white leather coat.

When he did so, Evangeline felt a hot liquid swirling around her neck and shoulders, growing hotter and tighter. She looked down—a beautiful, dense necklace of emeralds was forming. She grasped at it, but it was as though the molten necklace were electrified. Her hands sizzled with shock. After a few seconds, the mortal band had hardened and she could do nothing about it. It was as heavy as a boulder and stooped her spine.

"Not very nice, is it?" the king said. "I'll have it removed when you agree to bring your sister to me and reunite our family."

He made a dismissive gesture. Before Evangeline knew what was happening, the Lord High Keeper had snapped his ice-chunk fingers and the king's golden-armored bodyguards had surrounded her. Two of them picked her up by the elbows with no effort at all.

"With the power of the rootball stone, I will rule the Winter Kingdom as an immortal," King Vair said. "I only want to share that with you and your lost sister. Think about it. *Perhaps* you will come to your senses." He smiled, revealing sharp teeth like the Lord High Keeper's. "If not, you can only *hope* I will be merciful enough to let you rot in Bright Mine forever."

"You're a monster!" she barked at the king as the guards dragged her away, her bare feet squeaking on the smooth floor. King Vair shrugged wearily. Evangeline twisted and kicked, yelled and spat, but could not squirm from the grasp of the golden-armored guards; they might as well have been machines of unyielding steel. They whisked her toward the door to the throne room, armor clanking all the way.

Evangeline imagined the solitude of a dank, dark pit, her bones bent from the weight of the terrible mortal band. How could the king, that vile, sharp man, be her *father*? He was repulsive! She could still see the frightened face of the frozen page boy. No wonder her sister had run away. Evangeline didn't believe for a second King Vair wanted a heartwarming family reunion. But what was his real intention?

Evangeline had lived her whole life with someone whose secrets swirled just beneath the surface, and she saw the same murky calmness in the face of this winter king. He *needed* Desdemona and Evangeline for something. King Vair already lived in an opulent palace with more servants and soldiers than he could possibly remember, and could turn people to ice with one finger. But *immortality*—he'd used that word. Evangeline shuddered. The only good thing about terrible kings was that they eventually grew old and weak. What if this one never did?

She watched the king's unruffled, scowling face disappear beyond the tall door to the blue throne room. "I'll find you, Desdemona," she whispered. "I'll get us both out of here. Somehow."

❄ ❄ ❄

Once the king's bodyguards swept Evangeline back through the golden door, down the marble steps, past the blue soldiers, and out the massive palace gates, the Lord High Keeper thrust a clumsy portal into the air as he had done in Rime Village.

"Down the hill with her," he barked at the bodyguards. "There's a wagon leaving from the village any moment."

Evangeline could see a snow-nestled little town at the bottom of the heave of land upon which the great white palace sat. From here, the roofs were dull grays and greens, like mushrooms poking up from the white drifts. Through the greasy portal, she could see the same colors.

The two bodyguards carrying her by the elbows stepped purposefully toward the portal. "I'm not going anywhere!" Evangeline dug in her heels, scraping them on the gravelly road. But the golden-armored guards just marched through the hole in the air without even slowing down.

With the same rush and thump she'd felt on her first trip through one of the Lord High Keeper's doorways, Evangeline found herself on a muddy, busy street. Before her sat a heavy gray wagon parked in front of a lopsided gray building. The wagon was more like a solid wooden chest on wheels, and its padlocked door had thick iron bars in a little window at the top. Above the window was fastened a sneering iron gargoyle. At the front of the wagon, in the harness, she glimpsed the hindquarters of one of those remarkable cow-bear creatures she'd seen in Rime Village.

One of the golden-armored bodyguards whistled sharply. A helmeted head poked around the side of the wagon.

"What?" the driver said, squinting at the disappearing portal. His frizzy red hair poked from under his helmet and shook in the breeze. "Another one? One more minute and I'd have gone." He shuffled over and began clinking through a ring of keys on his belt.

The bodyguards said nothing, but when the driver had rattled open the padlock on the wagon door, he turned and peered at Evangeline from behind shaggy bangs. "That's—that can't be—"

"Open that door," a bodyguard snapped. "This one goes to the mine."

"This is a mistake!" Evangeline said. The bodyguard clapped a dirty hand over her mouth and squeezed as the driver squeaked open the wagon door. The stench of sweat and decay wafted from the gloomy, hay-strewn interior.

"No!" Evangeline tried to say, but her words were dampened by the bodyguard's meaty fingers. She tried to shake her head. She wriggled and lashed out with her legs. But this bodyguard was strong, and the other bodyguard was stronger. They pinned her arms to her sides, picked her up by her shoulders, and clamped some heavy iron shackles around her ankles. Then they tossed her into the prison wagon. Before she could scramble to her feet, the door slammed shut and she heard the heavy padlock clicking closed.

After a moment, the wagon lurched forward, with Evangeline bewildered and shivering in its foul darkness.

10

Evangeline could barely breathe. She climbed up onto one of the hard benches that lined the sides of the prison wagon, leaning forward so her head wouldn't smack the wall behind her as the wagon jolted along the frost-rutted road. Above her, the light from the gray winter day shone through the iron bars at the top of the door, almost dazzling to her sun-starved eyes, but just high enough to keep the benches in shadow. She closed her eyes. The prison wagon smelled like metal, rotten hay, and something else—it reminded Evangeline of the clear, pungent oil for the glass hurricane lamp her mom had kept under the sink in case the power went out.

But the dark, smelly, bumpy ride wasn't the worst of it. Neither were the shackles, whose heavy chain dangled between her feet, clanking with each bump in the road, or the emerald necklace that weighed on her shoulders. No, the worst thing was that Evangeline wasn't alone. There was another prisoner being taken to the mine.

She lowered her head and risked a peek to her left, where the bench she was seated on stretched deeper into the darkness. Someone else sat there, close enough to touch if she stretched out her arm. Just a shape in the shadows right now, motionless and silent. If she stared long enough, which she almost didn't dare, she thought she could make out the profile of a man. An enormous man with a hawk-beak nose and a wild nest of hair, sitting as still as the grave.

He didn't seem to be paying Evangeline any attention, although it was hard to tell. He could be looking sideways right now, too, as she was. Two strangers peering secretly at each other in the gloom.

What did he do to get arrested? Evangeline wondered. She squinted at the mountainous silhouette, just barely visible. *And is he guilty or innocent?* A lump of fear suddenly pushed on her throat. She swallowed. Would the king really have thrown her in here with someone dangerous?

She remembered the gray fire in his eyes as his quiet, angry words echoed in the throne room. *Yes.*

Evangeline squeezed her eyes shut, focusing instead on her sister. She tried to remember the details of her twin's face, her glossy hair, her diamond earrings. *Sister, I'm here*, she called in her mind. But she found nothing behind her eyelids but black.

The wagon gave a lurch, as though the two wheels opposite Evangeline had plunged into a ditch and out again. The heavy emerald necklace around Evangeline's neck jolted forward, and she was tossed onto the hay-strewn floor, the chain at her ankles clattering. The wagon lurched again, and she rolled. She got to her knees, hay sticking to her fingers, and looked back.

Now she was right in front of the huge man. She gasped at the sight of him, but he didn't even notice her crouched on the floor not two feet away. He was staring straight ahead, his eyes wide and his mouth downturned in an expression that was unmistakable, even in the shadows.

The huge, hawk-nosed prisoner was terrified.

And he was staring at something on the other side of the wagon. Something sitting on the other bench, in the farthest corner, cloaked in darkness. Something behind Evangeline.

Evangeline's breath was ice in her lungs. Part of her, the part that used to tell her to hide under the covers when she heard scary night noises, said that if she stayed perfectly still, the thing in the dark corner wouldn't notice her. The rest of her knew better. She knew whatever was hidden over there had watched her get thrown into the prison wagon by the golden-armored bodyguards, had seen her bounce onto the floor, and was probably looking at her right now.

Slowly, Evangeline turned her head until she could peer into the corner. At first, there didn't seem to be anything there. But after a few moments, her eyes adjusted to this deeper darkness, and she was able to make out a shape. Not a hulking presence like the man on the bench, but something—someone—small. Maybe taller than Evangeline, it was hard to tell, but as thin as an evening shadow. Then the wagon shuddered and winter light flashed across the corner just for a moment.

Evangeline's skin prickled. It was a person, maybe, but in the short moment the light crossed its face, the only things Evangeline could take in were its eyes. They were huge, with no irises, no white orbs, just wide and black and smooth like crystal balls. They were not human eyes.

Suddenly, the wagon jerked to a stop, sending Evangeline and her heavy chain tumbling headfirst into the sticky hay again. She was almost too afraid to sit up, but the floor of the wagon smelled so foul, she couldn't stand it. She uncurled, keeping herself small and quiet in the hay.

The door to the wagon gave a rattle and scrape as though someone were undoing the heavy iron padlock on the outside. At the sound, the big man broke his horrified gaze and whipped his head in the direction of the door. Evangeline looked, too. Had they arrived? What awaited them?

The door swung open and misty winter light flooded in. Evangeline squinted against the glare and put her forearm across her eyes. The wood floor creaked and swayed as someone with heavy boots stepped inside.

"Move it," Heavy Boots said, swishing Evangeline aside with his foot as though she were a clod of dirt. She scrabbled back to her bench, daring a peek through the open door as Heavy Boots—some kind of guard, she could see now—clomped past her. He wasn't as polished as the soldiers at the palace. His armor looked beat-up, not ceremonial, and his shoulders were stooped. How fast would those heavy boots carry him? Could Evangeline make a run for it?

There were two more guards just outside, with spiked helmets and big hands, plus the frizzy-haired driver. Was she fast enough to get by them?

Beyond the guards was a yard edged with a high wall made of large bricks of snow. The wall stretched away on both sides as far as Evangeline could see through the door. At the top, sharp-looking icicles of different sizes protruded at all angles. Directly in front of her was the thick wooden gate through which the wagon had come. It was made of tree trunks that had been carved into spikes at the top.

She gasped—the gate was still open! For a half second, Evangeline's insides sparkled with hope and nerves.

But then she saw what lay beyond the open gate: flat white nothingness. They were in the middle of a great plain, with only a single, great mountain stretching to the sky directly above the mine itself. If she made it past the guards, there was nowhere to go but miles through the snow, in plain sight, leaving tracks all the way.

It was hopeless. She let her shoulders fall back against the wall. Did she really expect to be able to escape from this prison? How could she ever help her sister now?

Heavy Boots had one thick-gloved hand thrust under the hawk-nosed man's elbow. "Get up, you," he said gruffly. "Come on, now. Welcome to Bright Mine, your new home."

"Just get me outta this wagon," the prisoner muttered. His feet were shackled, and the heavy chains left a trail through the hay as he lumbered toward the door. Evangeline watched him step down into the custody of the waiting guards, but he didn't look back once. His clothes were dirty and tattered in the sunlight, and hints of hard gray-white in his tangled hair and stubbly face reminded her of the Lord High Keeper, the great ice man with the sharp teeth.

Bright Mine. Evangeline peered out. Well, it was certainly bright. The sun off the white plain was relentless, turning the assortment of gray wooden structures nearby into painful blobs. Everywhere, ragged, shackled prisoners trudged over the packed snow, pushing unwieldy wooden carts full of hunks of dull crystal or hefting nasty-looking iron pickaxes. Rusty-armored guards watched them warily from under spiked helmets. Heavy Boots was speaking to a tall man with oiled green hair and long, pointed ears as they looked at a leather portfolio filled with yellow papers.

Evangeline pulled her legs up under her on the bench and curled into the shadows. The thing sitting in the corner of the wagon hadn't moved, but she felt it looking at her. It made the hair on the back of her arms tingle. She burned to steal a glance at it, now, in the light. At least she would know exactly what it was she was sharing a cell with.

With her heart thumping as loudly as the footsteps of the prisoners tramping by outside, Evangeline turned her face to the far corner of the prison wagon. The thing hunched there was bathed in light from the doorway, its dark crystal-ball eyes wide and bright.

It was a girl.

She looked older than Evangeline, maybe sixteen. She had dark hair, a pale face, and two shining, vicious fangs that reached all the way down her chin. Her arms—Evangeline shuddered; her heart nearly stopped—the girl had *four arms*, folded in her lap. They were very long and very thin, and completely covered in short, coarse black hair. All four of the girl's hands had long, hairy fingers whose white nails shone like polished eggshells.

That was Evangeline's first glance. Her eyes met the—the *spider-girl's*, and her skin went cold.

Then the spider-girl looked away. Down. She started picking at her dress. Evangeline blinked. There was something familiar about how the girl was acting. Evangeline recognized the routine. It meant, *I know you don't want to talk to me. So I'll pretend to be doing something else.*

Now Evangeline took her second look at the spider-girl. Four jet-black, hairy legs, each wearing a little white shoe, stuck out below the hem of her dress. The girl's four dainty ankles were shackled together with chains, just as Evangeline's were. Her dress was a worn, faded yellow, and even from here, Evangeline could see a few almost-matching patches sewn on with careful, awkward stitches.

Around her shoulders, the spider-girl wore a brown, threadbare shawl, which she pulled tighter as Evangeline watched.

Suddenly, with a wave of nerves, Evangeline realized that the way the spider-girl looked right now was the way Evangeline herself must look every time there was an empty seat next to her. Every time she sat there with her puffy coat pulled tight around her, waiting, *hoping*, that just one person would sit down and ask her name.

Evangeline knew what she had to do.

11

Summoning all her bravery, Evangeline rose. Her knees shook as she slowly took a couple of short steps across the hay-strewn floor of the prison wagon, her chain dragging. With a deep breath, she sat down next to the spider-girl and said, "Hi. My name's Evangeline. What's yours?"

The door slammed closed, draping Evangeline and the spider-girl in darkness once again. Evangeline waited, aching to poke at the silence with words, but she kept quiet.

Finally, a whispery voice said, "Hortense. My name is Hortense."

"Nice to meet you," Evangeline said, her voice just a little unsteady. "I'd shake your hand, but I can't see it."

A moment later, a faint blue glow started from Hortense's direction. Evangeline watched as she placed a small orb between them on the bench where it stuck and shone, illuminating the inside of the prison wagon with a light like the moon.

Two of Hortense's four thin, hairy hands reached out, their pearly fingernails gleaming in the strange blue light. Evangeline took a deep breath, then reached back to shake hands. But which hand to shake? She awkwardly stuck out both arms. They shook hands, two each. Hortense's fingers were strong and silky. Then they both laughed.

When Hortense laughed, her long fangs glistened. For a second, Evangeline's chest tingled with fear again. But she squashed the fear down and smiled. "Wow!" she said. "Did you have that glowing ball thing on you the whole time?"

Hortense nodded. "I didn't want to light it, though," she whispered, "I didn't want to see that frightening man."

"I don't blame you," Evangeline said, although she was surprised that someone like Hortense could be afraid of anyone.

Muffled voices surrounded them. It seemed more guards were surrounding the wagon. "So this is Bright Mine?" Evangeline said.

"Yes," Hortense said. "The king has the miners here—the prisoners—digging the crystals nonstop. It's dark and dangerous work. The tunnels are small and the ground can just shatter beneath you." She swallowed. "They say once you go in, you . . . you never come out."

"What a terrible place," Evangeline said, her stomach sinking. She tried to listen to the voices outside, but couldn't make anything out.

"It used to be beautiful," Hortense said. "Everything in the Winter Kingdom used to be beautiful." She seemed far away for a moment. Then she blinked, and looked at Evangeline. "Did you come from the capital city?"

"No," Evangeline said. "Or . . . yes? I came from the palace."

"The palace?" Hortense's wide eyes grew even wider.

Evangeline bit her lip, afraid she had revealed too much. "This huge man called the Lord High Keeper tossed me in here. He looked like he was—like he was made of ice or something."

"The Lord High Keeper!" Hortense gasped. "He's an ice troll. Mostly they herd cow-bears in the high mountains, but the Lord High Keeper is—different. Nasty. You *saw* him?"

Evangeline nodded. She couldn't imagine what Hortense would say if she told her she'd met the king, too. "It's a long story. The short version is that everyone thinks I'm someone else."

Now Hortense studied Evangeline's face. "Who are you?" she asked. But almost before the words were out of her mouth, Hortense's expression turned to one of surprise. "Oh!" she cried, falling to her knees in the sticky hay. "Your Highness! Forgive me—I did not know you in the shadows!" She covered her face with her delicate right forearms.

"No, stop!" Evangeline said, feeling her cheeks heat up.

Hortense peeked one shining eye over the top of an arm, then closed it again. "I don't understand, Your Highness."

"I'm not a Highness," Evangeline said, sliding off the bench and settling next to Hortense in the hay. She put a hand on one of her right arms. "I'm not even a Middle-ness. I'm nobody. I'm Evangeline, like I told you, and I came here looking for my sister. She's in trouble."

Hortense put her arms down. She looked at Evangeline cautiously. "What kind of trouble?"

"It's our father, King Vair," Evangeline whispered. "Desdemona refused to help him with something. He wanted her to—" Should she tell Hortense about the rootball, whatever that was? Evangeline wasn't sure how much she should reveal. "—to share in some big moment. She didn't want to. So she ran away."

Hortense shook her head. "I'm sorry. His Majesty is . . ." Her big black eyes swiveled, as though she were afraid of being overheard even in this wagon. "Well," she said. "I wouldn't like it if he were looking for *me*. People who anger him tend to . . . disappear."

"Right now, he still thinks I'm her," Evangeline said. "He's sending me to Bright Mine so I—she—can't escape again. The real princess Desdemona is hiding, but I don't know how long she'll be safe."

"You have to find a way out of here," Hortense said urgently. "You have to find the princess before King Vair realizes his mistake."

Evangeline swallowed. She thought of the garden of ice people.

"You must get your sister somewhere safe," Hortense said. "And yourself."

Earth, Evangeline thought. They would be safe there, beyond the mirrors. But how? "I don't know what to do," she said. "I just know I've been missing her my whole life, and now that she needs me, I don't even know where to start."

"I wish I could help you." Hortense gave a weak smile.

Evangeline felt a surge of warmth. "You do?" she said. It was the first time someone had wished they could help her.

Hortense nodded. "Well—there is one thing I can do." She raised two of her hairy black arms toward Evangeline's face. For a split second, Evangeline had to fight the instinct to jump back. Then Hortense slid her pearly fingernails underneath the heavy emerald necklace around Evangeline's neck and *pop!* It snapped open and fell into the hay with a soft thud.

"Thanks!" Evangeline said, astonished. "How did you know how to do that?" She picked up the band of emeralds, which now seemed as light as a necklace of feathers.

"It's a skill my people have had for generations," Hortense said proudly. "Not everyone can remove a mortal band. It's a closely guarded secret."

At that moment, footsteps crunched over the snow outside. Hortense grabbed the glowing blue orb and tucked it away. Evangeline tossed the mortal band under a bench. She could hear muffled voices, then the squeak of someone fiddling with the padlock.

"... not how we do things," muttered an oily voice Evangeline didn't recognize.

"I am not *interested* in how you do things," came the reply—a pompous little bark. "Do I need to remind you how much *paperwork* will be involved if you defy me? Because it will be *unfathomable* amounts of paperwork. Now, get that door open!"

Evangeline's heart sparkled just a little. She turned to Hortense and said, "I know that voice!"

12

Evangeline and Hortense leaned forward, listening through the door of the prison wagon.

The oily voice spoke again. "With all due respect, I was not informed that you required—"

"I am informing you right now!" the snooty little voice said. "I am a Keeper of the Crystal Gate and I wish to interrogate your prisoner *personally*, by order of the king himself. Open this door, driver." There was a pause, then the voice snapped, "At once!"

With a creak, the door of the prison wagon swung open. The official-looking green-haired man with the leather portfolio stood in the sunlight, squinting at a snow fox wearing an elaborately decorated purple-and-gold cape. Dragging her shackles, Evangeline hobbled over to the top of the rickety wagon steps. "Mr. Fox!"

The fox gave her a contemptuous look. "Sir *Paw*—" He paused, noticing her feet. "What, *what* is this?" he barked at the green-haired man. "You have the Princess of the Winter Kingdom in *chains*? Mr. Auditor, this is appalling!"

The green-haired man scowled. "All prisoners get—"

The fox pointed a white paw at the driver, who was trying to keep a low profile. "You! Get those off her at once!" He shook his head, muttering, "Chaining up royalty is not *allowed*; there isn't even a *form* for that!" Then he paused, looking skyward for a moment. "Well, perhaps a Form 916-B: Restraint of Precious Live Cargo for Transportation Purposes . . . but I'm not sure it would apply, and the number of signatures required would be astronomical . . ."

"Look, this isn't *regular*," Mr. Auditor said, but it was clear his heart wasn't in it.

Sir Paw-on-Stone gave him a stern look. "Fetch the commander immediately!" For a moment, the green-haired man looked like he might throw his leather portfolio right down into the packed, dirty snow, but instead he turned on his heel and strode off across the yard with the guards following.

Sir Paw-on-Stone turned to the driver. "And you had better produce the shackles key before I get peeved." When the driver hesitated, the snow fox barked, "Now!"

Grumbling, the driver began fishing around in a leather bag tied at his waist.

Sir Paw-on-Stone leaned toward the doorway where Evangeline stood, and she crouched to hear him. *"Be ready,"* he whispered.

"What?" Evangeline said. This fox changed moods faster than Jekyll and Hyde.

He rolled his eyes, which he seemed to do a lot, at least around Evangeline. *"When I tell you, you run. Run straight for the gate."*

Evangeline looked across the yard. Directly in front of her was the thick tree-spike gate through which the wagon had come. But now it was closed.

"Are you nuts?" she whispered. *"There's no way I can get that gate open."*

"I'll handle it," Sir Paw-on-Stone said, then barked, "Where's that key, man?"

"Keep your cape on," the wagon driver muttered. He stuck a smooth key into the shackles at Evangeline's ankles, and with a *click*, they popped open.

The driver eyed her suspiciously, but before he could say anything, the fox spoke up again. "Just *look* at the state of this wagon," he exclaimed. "These hinges are completely covered with rust! Why, this bolt is going to fall right off at any moment! I cannot let this wagon move another *inch* until these fittings are replaced." He made a scooting gesture with his paw. "Go along now and fetch your tools. I want this wagon in perfect working order!"

The driver frowned and crossed his arms. "Did you fall out of a tree? I'm not leaving these prisoners here with you! That arana in there will tear your head off!"

Evangeline worried Sir Paw-on-Stone had gone too far. But the fox steeled his gaze. "Excuse me?" he snapped. "Do you *dare* question my ferocity? I eat aranae for breakfast." He snarled and flashed his golden eyes. "And lippy wagon drivers for dessert!"

The driver's face went pale. "For—dessert?"

"With whipped cream on top!" the fox growled. "So tell me: Are you *refusing* to replace these rusty hinges?" He fluffed his fur, really getting into his role. "Is that what I'll tell the commander when your next batch of prisoners *escapes*?"

"All right, all right!" The driver put up his hands. "No need for that, sir." He scuttled off.

Sir Paw-on-Stone watched him go with an air of superiority. Then he gave Evangeline a deadly serious look. "The gate guards will change patrols in a few minutes. That's our opportunity. Wait for my signal, then flee."

Evangeline's breath quickened. "Listen, I'm not—"

"Zip it!" The fox blinked his golden eyes, then pointed to his lapel, where JELLY BEAN HUGS was still pinned. "This Terran brooch, your strange words and attitudes—it doesn't add up. You're the lost twin." He studied Evangeline's face. "Also, the real Princess Desdemona has pierced ears." Evangeline's hand flew to her ear. The fox leaned closer. "If you want to help your sister, we have to work together."

"But what should I do?" Evangeline asked. "How can I help her? What's going on?"

The fox spoke quickly. "These are dark days in the Winter Kingdom, Terra girl. Princess Desdemona and the other Keepers were the only people I could trust. I'm hoping I can trust you now."

"What do you mean they *were* the only people you could trust?" Evangeline asked.

The fox blinked. "I've just learned my colleagues Sir Quilted Wing and Madam Walks-Through-Walls have been killed. Lost at sea. Avalanche. Tragedy."

Those names . . . They pricked something in Evangeline's mind. Desdemona's list! She had been keeping track of these Keepers.

Sir Paw-on-Stone continued hurriedly. "That means ten Keepers of the Crystal Gate are now dead, all supposed accidents, which I don't believe for a moment."

"The Crystal Gate?" Evangeline asked in a hushed voice.

Sir Paw-on-Stone met her gaze with troubled golden eyes, then looked skyward. "It protects the Tree of Ancient Amethyst on the summit of this mountain—Bright Mountain. The tree contains immense power of life. We Keepers are the only ones with the power to pass through the gate."

"Power of life," Evangeline murmured. Then something wiggled in her mind. "Immortality."

The fox gave her a sharp glance. "What?"

"That's what King Vair said." Evangeline leaned close. "Something about a—what was it? A rootball."

Sir Paw-on-Stone's soft white fur bristled straight out like a toilet brush. He forgot himself for a moment and snapped, *"What?"*

Holding their breath, Evangeline and the fox scanned the yard for signs they had attracted attention, but the miners and guards went about their business as usual.

Evangeline lowered her voice. "What is a rootball?"

Sir Paw-on-Stone blinked slowly, annoyed, as though he'd been asked what color the sky was. He spoke in a hushed voice. "On the other side of the world from the Tree of Ancient Amethyst, at the highest peak of Mount Glory in the Summer Kingdom, grows the Tree of Ancient Topaz. The great roots of the two trees stretch down, down through mountains and earth, toward each other, until they come together at the center of the world. There they entwine, forming a mighty rootball, and within the rootball, the trees clutch their precious heart: the rootball stone." He scowled. "But the Keepers would *never* allow anyone to tamper with the rootball, not even the king."

Evangeline put her hand on the doorframe of the wagon. She looked up at the massive snowy peak looming above them, reaching into the clouds: Bright Mountain. "So the Tree of Ancient Amethyst is up there, behind the Crystal Gate," she said, "but its roots go all the way down . . . I think the king is *digging* for this rootball, here in Bright Mine. Could his miners be trying to reach the center of the world?"

Sir Paw-on-Stone's jaw opened. "It's *possible*, but—well, for one thing, it would take *years*. And even then, the Keepers of the Crystal Gate would put a stop to it."

"Unless someone got rid of them," Evangeline murmured.

Sir Paw-on-Stone looked at her, realization dawning. "I—you're right," he said sadly. "I didn't believe your sister when she suspected the Keepers were not merely unlucky as of late. I thought their deaths were just what they appeared. Food poisoning, a slip-and-fall, an unfortunate drowning—and the king seemed just as troubled about it as everyone else." He shook his head. "I wouldn't help her investigate. I wouldn't go with her when she begged me to escape before it was too late. I thought she was just being a foolish child. But now . . ." He paused. "Now it's clear King Vair has been behind it all."

"He wanted Princess Desdemona to find me and bring me here, but she refused," Evangeline said. "He says he wants the family to be united."

"Forgive me, but King Vair doesn't care about family," Sir Paw-on-Stone said, and Evangeline felt in her bones he was right. "He cares only about his own power and anything that would threaten it."

Evangeline frowned. "So why would he care about us?"

The fox took a sharp breath. "Of course—you and your sister are the only ones with a claim to the Sapphire Throne! If he's planning to live forever, you could be real thorns in his side." He clicked his tongue. "You'd be much more convenient as sculptures in his ice garden."

Evangeline's insides squirmed. "So the only reason I'm not a frozen dessert right now is because he thinks I'm her, and he needs *her* to get to—*me*." She gulped.

Sir Paw-on-Stone's eyes were somber. "For Desdemona's sake, I hope she has chosen an excellent hiding spot. You have fooled the king for now, but you won't be lucky for long. I can get you out of here, and then we must find Princess Desdemona at once. You must reach her, Evangeline, and bring her back to Terra, where King Vair cannot go. You have a connection to Terra. Your combined powers might be enough to create a portal between worlds."

I don't have any powers, Evangeline thought, startled at the suggestion. She didn't know anything about portals between worlds, or the Winter Kingdom, or this ancient tree and its stony heart.

But one thing she did know, in her own heart, was that her sister was in trouble. She shivered to think of King Vair storming into Desdemona's hiding place, shooting jets of ice from his fingertips. Sending her to Bright Mine forever—or worse, freezing her solid and putting her in the garden with all the other tragic, drippy ice people.

Evangeline *did* have a connection to Terra. And surely Desdemona was powerful like King Vair. Maybe that would be enough to bring them home. If Sir Paw-on-Stone thought Evangeline could save her sister, she would try.

The snow fox frowned. "If only we knew where she was hiding!"

Evangeline tried to pull herself together. She thought of the violet light that surrounded the princess when she vanished, and of the photographs, one on Earth and one in the Winter Kingdom. And she remembered the purple tree.

Purple tree! Evangeline raised her eyebrows. "I think she might have gone to the Tree of Ancient Amethyst itself."

Sir Paw-on-Stone's golden eyes widened. "Impossible! Unless— perhaps—" He thought for a moment. "If one of the other Keepers helped her . . . Yes, she would be safe there, as long as the Lord High Keeper didn't know . . ."

Evangeline's heart thudded. "Can you take me there?"

"Yes." The fox raised his head. "In fact, I alone can help you," he said, with a hint of arrogance. "I am the only one in all the Winter Kingdom who can open the Crystal Gate now, except for the Lord High Keeper himself." His eyes narrowed angrily. "Getting rid of the Keepers, leaving the tree unprotected, has been the king's plan all along. It will be dangerous."

"I have to try," Evangeline said, as bravely as she could. "Nobody's going to turn my sister and me into ice sculptures."

Suddenly, the painful whine of creaking metal cut the air just above them. Evangeline and Sir Paw-on-Stone whipped their heads around. The fox bristled. Evangeline's heart jumped against her ribs; she gasped at what she saw.

Above the door to the prison wagon, the ornamental iron gargoyle was *moving*. And it was moving quickly, uncurling its tail and stretching out its wings with horrible squeaks.

"A spy!" Sir Paw-on-Stone yelped. "Stop it!"

Evangeline threw her arms up and clumsily grasped at the metal talons, but the gargoyle pulled away and sprang from the roof of the wagon. In seconds, it was gone, flitting away over the white plain until it was a smudge, then a speck, then nothing.

"It will go straight to King Vair!" the white fox said, half growling. "It heard everything!"

Evangeline gaped at him. "What do we do?"

Sir Paw-on-Stone closed his eyes, his fur slowly smoothing back to normal. "The spy will reach the palace within the day, and tell the king not only that *you* are here in the Winter Kingdom, but also exactly where your sister is hiding. Neither of you is safe anymore."

"He'll find her!" Evangeline cried. "And me!"

Sir Paw-on-Stone nodded. "The Lord High Keeper will bring the king through the Crystal Gate by tomorrow. The Tree of Ancient Amethyst will surely try to protect the princess, but I fear it will not be enough. I—" He opened his golden eyes. "The guards are about to change patrol! Get ready to escape!"

"But what about the spy?" Evangeline cried. "Bring me through the Crystal Gate now!"

"The ritual to pass through the gate is complex. There isn't time!" The fox's eyes darted back and forth. "But—I can buy us a little." He closed his eyes, took a deep breath through his snout, and let out what Evangeline could only describe as an all-over sneeze. "Frrrrumph!" Sir Paw-on-Stone's white fur stood straight out, sparking with golden electricity, as a gust of wind or energy or magic—Evangeline couldn't tell which—rolled outward from his body and spread in all directions. Almost instantly, it was gone.

"Wow!" she said, staggering a little from the force. "What did you do?"

He shook his fur back into place. "I locked the Crystal Gate. Not even the Lord High Keeper can portal through it now."

"Then Desdemona is safe!" Evangeline breathed.

He shook his head. "If what you say is true, if King Vair has nearly reached the rootball stone, he will be able to use it to unlock the Crystal Gate."

"No . . . ," Evangeline murmured.

"But—" The white fox tapped a paw on the snow. "He will still be unable to portal there. He'll have to go on foot, along the Crystal Path, and that journey will take three days. So we have a little time, Terra girl, but we must work quickly. Your sister is safe, but she's also trapped. The lock works both ways." He looked toward the wooden gate. "It's time," he said urgently. "I will send you to a mountain some distance from here. There's a village called Oak at the bottom. Meet me at the tavern. Then I shall undo my lock and send you through the Crystal Gate to your sister."

"What about Hortense?" Evangeline asked.

"Hortense?" Sir Paw-on-Stone frowned, one ear flopping over. "Who's Hortense?"

Evangeline gestured to where her new friend sat hunched in the corner of the prison wagon.

The fox blinked. "You want to free an *arana*? Now who's nuts?"

There was something about how Sir Paw-on-Stone said it that reminded Evangeline of her mother. She raised her chin at him. "I'm not leaving Hortense behind. Not in this awful place."

"Look." The fox put his front paws on the doorsill. His voice was urgent. "There's no *time*. The new guard patrol will be here any moment to take over. Not to mention the driver with his tools."

"But," Evangeline said. "But what about all the growling, and whipped cream—"

"I'm *saving you*," the fox interrupted. "Don't let me regret it!"

"I won't." Evangeline bent down and pulled the shackles off from around her ankles. Then she extracted the key and dashed back to where Hortense was seated. "This will just take a second . . ."

"They're coming!" Sir Paw-on-Stone yelped. "And there's Mr. Auditor and the commander! You must go now!"

"Go," Hortense whispered, a sob in her voice, as Evangeline fumbled with the lock at her feet. "Go, Evangeline."

"No," Evangeline said. "You've already saved my butt once. We're going together."

Click. Hortense's shackles swung open. "Come on!" Evangeline cried. "Come with me." She scampered to the doorway. They had a chance—a moment—but how could they possibly escape?

Then she saw the snow fox, his eyes closed in deep concentration. His white fur blazed like fire, a star fallen to earth. Beyond him was the fearsome wooden gate. Only now, there was something strange about it. It shone, unstable and flickering, almost as though its molecules were flapping in the breeze. And even from here, Evangeline could see the hint of a reflection in its formerly dull surface.

A portal! Sir Paw-on-Stone was creating a portal, just like the Lord High Keeper had done.

And just in time. He was right—she saw the shape of the frizzy-haired wagon driver and two pointy-helmet guards coming from one direction, and oily-voiced Mr. Auditor approaching from the other way, accompanied by someone taller, with an even pointier helmet.

"What do we do?" Hortense asked timidly. She had a long bag slung over her back and looked worriedly at Evangeline.

Evangeline's mind churned. If they could run fast, *fast*, to the gate, if they could *get through* into whatever place was beyond, if they could *hide*, if, if, *if* . . .

"You!" a voice boomed. The commander. Evangeline saw him quicken his steps, pointing at Sir Paw-on-Stone, who was so lost in his magic he didn't even seem to be breathing.

"I'm not a runner," Evangeline said. "I'm not good at running." She had almost forgotten.

"You must be," Hortense said, putting a hand on Evangeline's arm.

At that moment, another pointy helmet thrust itself into the doorway of the prison wagon, inches from Evangeline and Hortense. It sat atop the head of a particularly menacing-looking guard with a broken tooth. "What's going on here?" he roared. Evangeline almost fell over. The guard noticed Sir Paw-on-Stone. "Hey! No magic here!" He pulled a heavy-booted foot back and aimed at the little fox's midsection.

"No!" Evangeline yelped. She gave the guard a *push*, as hard as she could, and he staggered backward three steps.

The guard's face turned into a thunderstorm of anger as he rushed forward toward Evangeline and Hortense in the prison wagon. He was strong and fast. Evangeline's heart sank. None of the fox's tricks mattered. They'd never make it to the gate.

Then, to Evangeline's astonishment, Hortense lunged at the guard, fangs glistening.

"HISSSS!"

It was the most spine-chilling sound Evangeline had ever heard in her life. The guard cried out and recoiled. Evangeline leapt out of the wagon and pushed him square in the chest. He fell over. The short way from the wagon to the gate was clear.

Evangeline and Hortense ran.

13

By the time Evangeline heard the first "Hey!" from an alarmed guard, she was already at the wooden gate, which shimmered and rippled with Sir Paw-on-Stone's portal magic.

She didn't have time to worry. All she could do was barrel toward the portal, the only thing around that looked even a little bit like freedom. Inches from the wall of thick, pointed logs, Evangeline pressed her eyes closed, lowered her head like a charging rhinoceros, and *leapt* . . .

There was a rush of cold air, that stomach-flipping feeling of up-down-sideways, and then the gate melted away and she was racing out the other side. She skidded down a steep, rutted road, bounding, flying like a deer into the thick, frosty forest that clung to the side of a mountain that her brain insisted hadn't been here a moment ago.

She risked a look backward. At the sight of the terrifying thing on her tail, she almost fell over—until she realized it was only Hortense.

She seemed more spider than girl as she ran, using all eight legs, which stretched and stretched in all directions.

At first, the snow in this Winter Kingdom seemed just like the snow in Lakecrest and Greenfield and all the other places Evangeline and her mother had lived. It was white and cold and fell in big, gentle flakes from the gray sky. But there was something different about it, too. As soon as Evangeline's bare feet touched down, she felt a surge of—of *something*, shooting up through her legs, like power erupting from the snow itself. It filled her with what she could only think of as a glorious *coldness* as she sprinted across the white ground.

It looked like a couple of mine guards had managed to leap through the portal after them, but they were falling away in the distance, shouting and sliding as they ran. Far in front of them, Hortense scuttled so quickly she was nothing more than a blur over the snow.

Evangeline kept running. She had never moved like this in all her life. She wasn't particularly good at gym class, and of course her mother never let her try out for sports. But now, here, she felt invincible. She felt like an astronaut in those videos of the moon landing, springing high and far. Only instead of slow, relaxed space bounces, she propelled herself at incredible speed through the frigid daylight. Each footfall, pushing off the glittering snow, carried her farther through the air as the ground whizzed by.

At last, when she felt tall trees crowding safely all around her, she tumbled to a stop, ducking behind the large trunk of a fat pine. Cautiously, she poked her head around the side of the tree and listened. She strained her ears, ringing with the cold air and the pounding of her blood.

Nothing. Where was Hortense? Had the guards caught her? Evangeline's heart sank.

But then she heard the *scritch-scritch-scritch* of eight legs scurrying over the snow, and soon Hortense skidded to a stop next to her among the trees.

"I think we made it!" Hortense said, out of breath. "Oh, how you can *run*!"

"Who knew?" Evangeline said, grinning. *I certainly didn't*, she thought. She patted two of Hortense's shoulders, awkwardly draped in her windblown shawl, and sank back into the snow behind the tree.

Hortense plopped down next to her, and they rested their heads against the rough bark. "What now?" she asked. "I—I don't really have anywhere to go. I'm from the village of Gnashing, far from here. Or— far from Bright Mine. I don't know where 'here' is anymore."

"The nearest village is Oak," Evangeline said. "Sir Paw-on-Stone said he'd meet me there. I've got no time to lose—that creepy little gargoyle is on its way to blab to King Vair right now. Then he'll know where my sister is." It felt like they'd run for miles, but the ground beneath them still tilted. They weren't even at the bottom of whatever mountain the portal had spat them out onto.

"Sir Paw-on-Stone?" Hortense furrowed her brow. "Is he the fox who works for the king? Are you sure you can trust him?"

It was a precarious situation, Evangeline had to admit. But she said, "I think so. I don't have a choice really. I don't have a lot of options. Besides, he's in danger, too. The Keepers of the Crystal Gate have been dropping like flies, and he has to be next."

"The Keepers? Oh no!" Hortense put two hands to her mouth.

"Sir Paw-on-Stone and the Lord High Keeper are the only ones left," Evangeline said. "Ten gone out of twelve."

"Out of thirteen," Hortense said darkly. "King Vair had the aranae Keeper executed twelve years ago when he kicked the aranae out of Bright Mine." Then she gasped, looking at something in the distance. "Evangeline! Do you see that cave in the cliff over there? Look at the trees around it—are those orbs hanging from the branches?"

Evangeline peered in the direction Hortense was looking, but the cliff was hard to make out. "I'm not—" she started, but was interrupted by a loud *thwack!* She and Hortense both jumped to their feet.

"What . . . ?" Hortense said.

It was then, with an even louder *thwack!*, that the second crossbow bolt buried itself in the tree next to them. And this one struck even closer to their heads.

14

"**The mine guards! Run!**" Evangeline yelled as another deadly bolt zinged by them into the forest. She and Hortense leapt and staggered through the heavy snow, ducking behind trees, zigging and zagging.

There were shouts behind them, but Evangeline didn't turn around. They were heading toward the cliff cave Hortense had seen. Could they hide there? Could they even reach it?

Hortense struggled to keep up. The snow was deeper here than up higher on the mountain and she had twice as many legs to get caught in it.

Evangeline grabbed one of Hortense's hands. "We have to get to the cave," she said, pulling her along.

"Okay," Hortense said. But a moment later, she let out a cry. Her hand jerked out of Evangeline's grasp.

Evangeline slid to a stop and turned back. "Hortense!"

There was a crumpled shape in the snow. Black arms and legs askew, with one white shoe thrown off to the side. And a crossbow bolt sticking out from a yellow dress.

Evangeline threw herself down next to Hortense as the mine guards gained ground.

"Aaaargh!" Hortense wailed, grimacing.

"Don't move!" Evangeline said, pulling the brown shawl from where it lay nearby and draping it over Hortense. The crossbow bolt was dull gray metal, as big around as Evangeline's pointer finger. Should she pull it out or leave it in? Oh, *why* hadn't her mother let her take First Aid?

"Ungh!" Hortense opened her shiny black eyes. "It's my shoulder. I . . . can't get up. You've got to get away." She jerked her four knees up to her chest, curling up from the pain.

"I won't let the guards get you." Evangeline put a hand on one of Hortense's good shoulders.

"They're not . . . guards," Hortense said weakly. "The guards didn't have crossbows."

"What? Then who?" Evangeline could hear the crunch of footsteps now. Whoever had been firing at them was closing in.

"It's down!" a voice called. "I can see it!"

What a strange thing to say, Evangeline thought. Moments later, a man appeared. He was wearing snowshoes and a thick coat, with a crossbow slung across his back. "Over here!" he called.

Evangeline watched him warily. Hortense was right—this man wasn't wearing a pointy guard helmet. "Why did you shoot at us?" she called back.

Two more people, a man and a woman, joined him, moving slowly over the snow. All three were very tall and thin, with long necks, long faces, and dark, wide-apart eyes. Each one had two short, knobby horns, and a long tongue that curled when they opened their mouth. They reminded Evangeline of giraffes.

"Told you I saw an arana," the man said to the others. "In our woods!"

"Is that a human girl?" the woman asked. "Are you all right?" she said to Evangeline.

"Leave her," the second man butted in. "She was obviously traveling with it." The tall people were keeping their distance.

Hortense groaned, moving slightly in the snow. A red patch was beginning to soak into the white around her.

"My friend needs help!" Evangeline cried. "Please."

The first man spat on the ground and pointed to Hortense. "Tell it to scream for help from its nestmates! And you can join them, for all I care!" He raised his crossbow again. Evangeline's heart jumped in fear. But then something else happened—a tingle started inside, at her center. A shivery, electric feeling that zapped through her tissue . . .

BOOM!

For a split second, the forest *lurched* as though someone had given the world a kick, and the sky flashed a blinding purple. The giraffe-like people were knocked to the ground and Evangeline was tossed onto her back. Had she . . . ? *No*, she realized. *It wasn't me who did that*. Then part of her wondered why she'd even considered the possibility.

"What the sneeze was that?" said the crossbow man in a shaky voice as he got to his feet.

"It came from Bright Mine!" the woman said.

Bright Mine. Evangeline's guts shivered. *The rootball stone. King Vair's miners have reached it*. The knowledge didn't come from her own thoughts. It was as though the forest itself whispered it word-lessly all around her. Now the king had the power to unlock the Crystal Gate and reach Desdemona. All he had to do was get there—and it would only take three days.

"Come on, let's get out of here," the crossbow man said to the others. "It's two miles back to Oak and getting dark."

All three of the giraffe-like people turned to go. Evangeline's stom-ach sank as she watched them tramp away through the trees. "You can't leave us here!"

But they never looked back.

Evangeline slumped next to Hortense and put a hand on her forehead. It felt . . . normalish? She wasn't sure what temperature an arana's forehead was supposed to be. "Who needs those weirdos, anyway?" she said, trying to keep her voice steady. "All they wanted to do was shoot us with crossbows."

Hortense gave a frail laugh. "I think you're right!" She coughed wetly. "Listen," she said, pointing. "If you can get to that cave, you will find help. I know it."

Evangeline could just see the cave through the trees. High and dark. It gave her a chill. "What's in there?"

"My people," Hortense murmured. "I do not know them, but there are aranae there, I am sure." She pulled the little orb from her pocket and handed it to Evangeline. "To light the way—see." She passed a hand over it and it started glowing the way it had in the prison wagon. With another pass of her hand, the orb went dark again, and she handed it to Evangeline. It felt like a pool ball covered in silk, only light as a cork. When Evangeline waved her fingers over its surface, it shone.

"Very good!" Hortense said. Then she let her head fall back into the snow.

Evangeline darkened the orb and put it in her pocket. In the distance, the cave was still and silent. *And full of aranae*, Evangeline reminded herself with a shudder. Could she do this? Could she just go skipping into a dark cave full of spider-people? It wasn't a situation she would have ever thought she'd be in.

Hortense adjusted herself with a painful grimace.

Evangeline felt the pang of guilt. "This whole thing's my fault," she said. "If I hadn't convinced you to escape with me, if I hadn't tried to make a friend . . . Maybe Mom was right."

"Your mother isn't here, and this isn't Terra," Hortense said, raising her head a little. "You're so brave, my friend Evangeline. I know you will be brave enough."

Evangeline smiled. "Wow. Nobody's ever called me brave before."

"You're a *taranta*!" Hortense said. "A warrior!" She gave a gurgling cough and swallowed.

Evangeline inhaled the ashy winter air. To her surprise, she wasn't even cold. She could *feel* the cold, but it didn't bother her. In a strange way, it was like brushing her teeth—fresh, cool, exciting, but not uncomfortable—only not just inside her mouth, but all over and through her body. She had minty blood.

She wasn't afraid of the winter here. In fact, it was exhilarating.

Suddenly, small at first but growing, Evangeline felt a tingle in her legs where they rested in the forest snow. It was a chill through her corduroys, but it whispered, too. It was alive. Then she felt it on her forehead—sparks of icy energy that leapt from the crust and crawled over her skin.

"All right, Hortense," she said, getting to her feet. "Sit tight and keep warm. Here, wrap up in this." She pulled her fuzzy white sweater over her head and draped it over Hortense's thin body.

"You'll freeze!" Hortense said, gaping at Evangeline's bare arms sticking out through the sleeves of her T-shirt.

Evangeline breathed in the scents of pine and snow. It was like jumping into a pool. At first, the cold seemed shocking, but after a few moments, she realized she was just fine.

"No," she said. "I won't."

She set off toward the cliff and the dark cave. The sooner she got there, the sooner she could bring help back for Hortense.

❄ ❄ ❄

The cliff was farther than it looked. Evangeline trudged on, passing tree after dark tree, boulder after jutting boulder. Soon the sun began to dip, casting long blue shadows across the white ground. A stream bubbled along beside her, too excited for the ice to grow thick.

Something made Evangeline pause by the stream. She stared into the lively water. Her reflection was barely recognizable. It looked more like a cluster of shining, wiggling worms, never quite making a whole picture. Still, she called out, quietly: "Sister?" Nothing. No eyes staring back. No images of the purple tree growing out of the cracked boulder. "Desdemona," she whispered, concentrating.

And there, suddenly, beyond the water, was Princess Desdemona! The ripples calmed, and Evangeline saw her sister sitting cross-legged on the ground. A diffuse purple light surrounded her.

She looks okay, Evangeline thought with relief. "It's me, Evangeline," she said, louder this time. "Sister! It's me!"

Evangeline saw her sister raise her head and look around, startled. Princess Desdemona scrambled to her feet, looking every which way. "Evangeline?" The sound of her voice was echoey and far, but it was there.

"Yes!" Evangeline said. "I'm here! I'm in the Winter Kingdom!"

"You should not have come!" Princess Desdemona cried. "I was wrong!" She wrung her hands and turned this way and that, trying to find out where Evangeline's voice had come from.

For a moment, Evangeline agreed with her sister. *You shouldn't be here*, she thought, with a voice that sounded like Mom's. *It's far too dangerous. You know nothing about this place or its magic. You're in over your head.*

But she couldn't let Princess Desdemona see how worried she was. Not when King Vair's forces were looking for them both; not when the king himself would reach Desdemona's hiding spot in only three days.

So Evangeline steeled her voice. "You're in the tree, right?" she called. "The Ancient Amethyst?"

"Yes," Desdemona said, which made Evangeline puff with pride at her own detective skills. "But you must go back! Listen—Father must not discover who you are!"

"I'll be careful," Evangeline called back. Her sister's terrified face tugged at her heart, but she had to warn her. "You're safe for now," she said. "Don't try to leave the tree—Sir Paw-on-Stone has sealed it to protect you. I'm coming, sister. I'm coming to bring you home to Earth!"

"Go back!" Princess Desdemona shouted, though it was as faint as a whisper. "You mustn't . . ." And she faded.

"Sister!" Evangeline hissed. "Desdemona!" But there was no response. Just her own reflection looking back at her.

There was no way she'd go back without Desdemona, even if she could.

But she also couldn't abandon Hortense, bleeding in the snow. Evangeline rose and followed the stream, keeping her eyes fixed on the cliff cave, her steps quicker now. Still, it felt like she was crawling toward it at a snail's pace.

A strange shape to her left caught her attention. She stopped and peered up into the branches of a spreading tree. There was an orb hanging there, sort of like the one Hortense had given her, but much bigger. A sign of the aranae! Evangeline almost clapped her hands. She couldn't have far to go now.

Sure enough, she could see the base of the cliff just beyond this last, thick clump of trees. And as she moved, half staggering, half running through the snow, she saw more and more of the big white orbs. They dangled from branches high and low like wasps' nests.

She passed very close to one that hung just at shoulder height. Unlike the warm, silken ball in her pocket, this thing looked rough and wet. Evangeline reached out her fingers. The surface was sticky, like some kind of super-slimy rubber cement. She touched it. Her fingertips stuck—the orb didn't want to let go.

With a horrified cry, Evangeline jerked her hand back. Her fingers came away with a *pop!* and she almost fell over. The strange white orb shuddered.

Now she looked around her into the thick forest, glowing with the champagne light of evening. The orbs surrounded her on every side. Evangeline held her breath. The forest was silent here. No birds, no chittering squirrels, just hundreds of hanging orbs, lumpy and dripping like bloated heads.

Evangeline hurried on, keeping her eyes on the ground in front of her. She slid sideways when the trees grew too thick, careful not to touch any more orbs.

At last, she came to the base of the cliff and looked up. It was a steep climb to the jagged entrance of the cave, over great hunks of quartz and tipped-up tables of shale. And all along the way were more of the large orbs, stuck onto the side of the cliff like wads of old gum. It didn't feel like a place where she would find help.

In the silence, Evangeline remembered the stricken face of the hawk-nosed man in the prison wagon. She thought of the three giraffe-like people, who'd been unconcerned with Evangeline but desperate to bring down her friend. She thought of Sir Paw-on-Stone's shocked words: *You want to free an* arana?

Who is Hortense, really? she wondered as she clambered over the rocky path that led up, up, up to the mouth of the cave. *And why was she in the prison wagon to begin with?* Evangeline realized she had never asked. *What crime did Hortense commit?*

Evangeline pulled herself up over the final ledge and found herself face-to-face with the hole in the side of the cliff. Wisps of webbing floated in the breeze, reaching toward her from the depths. Stale air with hints of moss and mushrooms and old bones wafted out from the darkness.

As Evangeline peered into the cave, she realized she didn't really know Hortense at all.

15

The low sun stretched its golden fingers into the cliffside cave.
Evangeline could see a well-worn dirt path leading away and curving sharply out of sight. The sides of the path were littered with twigs, stones, and leaves. More sticky orbs dotted the walls here and there along the way.

She took a step inside. The unsettled, earthy cave air pushed strands of her hair back from her forehead. At first, the cave seemed just as quiet as the forest below. But as Evangeline paused, listening, something echoed in the gloom, farther along the path. Drips, scratches, thuds. Muffled noises that could be the wind through a crack in the stone, or voices, or notes of mystical music.

Evangeline crept along the path until she reached the place where it curved into darkness. *What are you doing?* she asked herself. *You came to the Winter Kingdom to find your sister, not go exploring in creepy caves!* Every nerve, every neuron, every fiber in her, every raised hair on her arms screamed, *No! Turn back!*

But she knew Hortense was out there in the snow, growing colder and colder. *You barely know her*, Evangeline told herself, only it sounded like her mother's voice in her head. *Why were the guards after her in the first place? What if she's a con artist? Or a spy? Or a murderer?*

"Maybe she is," Evangeline murmured. "But she's also hurt and alone right now. I can't just turn my back on her." Was that what Mom would do? She wasn't sure. But she kept moving forward, following the twists in the dirt path until she'd left the golden sun-fingers behind.

Suddenly, something cold and bony thrust itself out of the shadows. It grabbed her shoulder. Evangeline cried out, but the thing hung on, digging into her sweater. "Let go!" she shrieked, wrenching away. She pressed her back against the rock wall, her breath coming ragged.

In the dim light, she could make out the shape of a skeletal hand— the thing that had grabbed her. It wasn't moving now. Hesitantly, she took a step toward it. Still nothing. Another step. She reached out, pressing one of her fingers to the pale bones . . .

It was a root.

Evangeline laughed and leaned back against the cave wall.

"Who's there?" came a muffled voice from farther in, around a corner. The voice was thin and grating, a whisper across rusty nails.

Aranae!

For a moment, Evangeline was afraid. Even though she had come here looking for the spider-people, the idea of meeting them face-to-face was frightening. She glanced back. If she bolted, she could duck around the twists in the path and be outside before the voice and who-ever it belonged to saw her.

I'm here for Hortense, she reminded herself. So, summoning the courage Hortense seemed to think she had, she called out, "I'm Evangeline Reynolds. I need help. I'm looking for the aranae."

Someone stepped into view. "You've found them," the figure said, just as two more emerged from the depths of the cave.

At that moment, everything was flooded with white-blue light, as though the cave were a glass of water that someone suddenly dropped the moon into. Dust and wisps of web in the air glittered. And there, before Evangeline, stood three scowling aranae.

They wore gleaming armor plates on their chests and long robes that were ornately decorated but shiny and worn in places. They looked like soldiers. All three of them towered over Evangeline. They were even taller than the Lord High Keeper.

One of them stepped forward. She had two of her slender, hairy arms on her hips and the other two were crossed. She stared down at Evangeline with her dark crystal-ball eyes. The blue-white cave light glinted off fangs that were as long as Evangeline's hand from palm to fingertip.

"What trickery is this, Your Highness?" the head soldier hissed. She clicked her tongue, which Evangeline found particularly unsettling. "Hasn't your father done enough to the aranae?"

Evangeline tried to stand up straight, but it was hard with three spider-people glowering down at her. "I'm not the princess," she said in her bravest voice, "and I'm not trying to trick you. Please believe me."

One of the other soldiers gave her a puzzled look. He leaned in to the leader. "What should we do, taranta?"

Taranta. Warrior, Evangeline remembered. She gulped.

The taranta uncrossed her arms. She swept a dismissive gesture in Evangeline's direction. "We repay King Vair for what he has done to us. Death."

"What? No!" Evangeline shrieked. The towering aranae moved like lightning. All of a sudden, one was behind her, blocking the path back to the cave entrance. Two slender arms shot out and dug fingernails like needles into Evangeline's shoulders. "I need *help*, not *death*!" she cried. "Death is the *opposite* of help! My friend Hortense—"

Her words were cut off by a sticky cloth that suddenly covered her mouth. *No*, she realized, *not a cloth*. It was the white substance the orbs were made of. Now she knew what it was: spider silk. The taranta's mouth was open, and silk was shooting from behind her shining fangs, sticking to Evangeline's face, shoulders, and arms.

Evangeline struggled as the other aranae twisted her around like a bobbin getting wound with thread. The spider silk soon wrapped her up from head to toe, with only a small gap for her eyes and nose. She was utterly stuck.

"Bring her to the Center," the taranta said. One of the others scooped Evangeline up and threw her over his shoulder as though she were no heavier than a sausage, which was just about what she felt like. She squirmed, but he held on. Those thin arms were as strong as steel.

Deeper into the cave they went, the three aranae soldiers swiftly scuttling through the lattice of passageways. Evangeline couldn't see much except for the ground slipping away beneath her in the bright, moon-colored light.

Death. Were they really going to execute her? How?

Evangeline shuddered. She knew exactly how spiders killed their victims. Step one: catch them in the web. Step two: wrap tightly in silk. Step three . . . she didn't want to think about it. All she could see in her mind were those long, shiny fangs.

They came to what felt like a large, open space filled with the sounds of voices. Evangeline managed to twist her upper body a little bit this way and that to get a better look. They were in a vast clearing or pit. Rock walls still rose up on all sides, but the air was different here—fresher. Evangeline knew if she could flip all the way over, she'd see a sunset sky overhead. This must be the Center the taranta had mentioned.

Round huts with round windows were stacked like piles of muddy marshmallows. Aranae went unhurriedly about their business, with many seated at cozy tables sipping from beer steins or laughing with their long legs dangling over the backs of vacant chairs. Unlike the hustle and bustle of Rime Village square at midday, this village-in-a-cave had settled into a relaxing evening. Evangeline almost wished she could join them.

Except that, well, they wanted to execute her. She saw two aranae dressed in grubby overalls clinking mugs in a toast. *What are they toasting, a human sacrifice?* she wondered suspiciously. *And what's in the mugs? Probably blood.*

The air became closer as they moved into someplace sheltered. The arana carrying her trotted up some stairs, Evangeline's head bouncing with the movement. Then, *thud!* He heaved her forward over his shoulder and let her slide heavily onto a tiled floor.

"Ow!" Evangeline said, but it came out more like, "Mmph!" *There has to be a way out of this*, she thought, thinking of poor Hortense alone in the snow, a crossbow bolt sticking out of her. If the aranae wouldn't help, Evangeline had to escape. She had to try to reach Oak, the village Sir Paw-on-Stone had mentioned, and she had to get there fast.

If only she had a jackknife in her pocket! She remembered *that* conversation, when her grandmother had sent her that gorgeous silver knife with the mother-of-pearl inlays and the swan etched into the blade. Mom had taken it away at once— *Ugh, what do you need that fancy thing for?* she'd said. *We have good scissors and a whole set of kitchen knives from Super Mart. No need to show off.* Evangeline wondered if the little swan knife would have cut through this spider silk and helped her escape. Now she would never know.

She wiggled to a sitting position and looked around. She was in a long room made of diamonds and lit with rainbows. Just to her left, a waterfall cascaded down the wall and through a crevice in the shining floor. It was so beautiful that Evangeline forgot her panic for a moment.

But just for a moment. The three soldiers who'd captured her were standing directly in front, blocking her view of what might have been a raised platform at the end of the room, in front of a wall of brightly embroidered tapestries. The aranae were speaking, but Evangeline couldn't make out what they were saying through the silk in her ears. They weren't paying Evangeline any attention for the moment.

Now might be her chance to—to flop her way out of here. She twisted around, studying the room through the slit in her wrappings, dazzled by the diamond walls and rainbow light. No—it wasn't diamond that lined the walls after all. It was quartz, thick and smoky, just like she'd seen outside the entrance. And the rainbows were—could it be? The multicolored light that danced across the crystals was coming from the orbs. They were stuck to the walls here, just as they had been on the path earlier and in the woods outside. Those sticky, bloated orbs that had made Evangeline so nervous were just . . . lights?

Then she realized: The crevice into which the waterfall was pouring looked just big enough for her to slip through. And it was only a few feet away.

As quietly as she could, she began to worm her way across the floor, inch by inch. Soon she was close enough to slide her face out over the hole. Droplets from the rushing water splashed into her eyes, but she could tell it was a long tumble into darkness. Still, there had to be some kind of pool at the bottom, right?

And just how are you going to avoid sinking like a stone? she asked herself. But her question was answered when she felt the wrappings around her eyes and nose loosen. The water was dissolving the silk, and quickly! If she could manage to not drown for just a minute when she hit the water, she could wriggle the wrappings off. And despite her mother's refusal to sign her up for swimming lessons, Evangeline was a good swimmer. She was a natural.

This could work.

Slowly, she edged herself farther and farther over the lip of the crevice. The mist from the waterfall felt cool on her face, which was almost completely free of silk now. She took a huge gulp of air—it was going to have to last her awhile—and kicked herself into the hole.

At that moment, four strong hands grasped her ankles and pulled her, writhing and gasping, back up into the rainbow-lit room.

16

"Get back here," a scratchy voice said. Evangeline was dragged once again into the center of the room, with the three aranae soldiers looming over her with fierce expressions. The one pulling her deposited her just in front of the platform at the end, where more aranae were gathered, looking down. A few sat on glossy wooden stools; fewer stood in the back wearing wooden expressions and thick armor.

At the center, a lavishly dressed arana sat on a slab of polished quartz as big as a refrigerator. This queen, or president, or whatever she was, wore a tall crown of bent brass spikes. Her once-black hair was streaked with gray that striped the eight long braids that fell over her shoulders. Her arms and legs were dotted with gray jaguar spots. She leaned to one side with two of her legs crossed over the other two, staring intently at Evangeline.

"Well, well," she said in a low voice that sounded like silk being stretched over fingernails. "Desdemona, Princess of the Winter Kingdom."

But Evangeline's mouth was free now, too. All of a sudden, her words blasted forth. "I am *not* Princess Desdemona of the Winter Kingdom! I am *Evangeline Reynolds* from *Earth*."

The head arana's huge black eyes widened in surprise. The four strong hands holding Evangeline in place tightened their grip like a warning.

Evangeline's heart was beating, *thup-thup-thup*, as though she were afraid, but she didn't feel afraid anymore. She thought of Hortense, waiting for help while her own people did nothing. "I am tired of being tossed around this kingdom like a sack of potatoes," she snapped. "I am sick of trying to do the right thing and being kicked and manhandled every step of the way." *Thup-thup-thup* went her heart. *Whooooosh* went her sparkling, chilly blood. "And I am *sick* and *tired* of saying *this is who I am* to people who will not listen!"

Suddenly, she felt herself explode. *Crack!* It was like every tiny hair on her body had turned into a cold, sharp pin and launched itself from her skin. For a split second, she thought all her blood had come shooting out of her pores and nothing would be left of her but a pile of dry bones.

Then she realized the spider silk that had been wound around her was . . . gone. She looked down. The wrappings lay in icy shards on the smooth floor. Some of them were sliding away in all directions. The cocoon that had imprisoned her had snap-frozen and splintered away, as though it were nothing more than a piece of delicate sugar icing being crushed in a hand.

The room was totally silent for a moment. The head arana stared with a look of shock on her pale face. Then the three soldiers who had captured Evangeline regained themselves and drew long, thin, curved swords from their backs. More armed arana soldiers joined them in a flash. Evangeline made another lunge at the dark gap in the floor, but the soldiers surrounded her, wrapping her in sword points instead of silk.

She was stuck again, just as stuck as she'd been in that sticky cocoon.

The head arana craned her neck. She tilted her head in a puzzled way. "Why do you keep trying to jump down that hole?"

Evangeline blinked. "Why—what?"

The head arana shrugged. "It doesn't look very safe, does it? I don't even know what's down there." She turned to the aranae seated next to her. "Do we know what's down there?"

"Some kind of drain?" an arana wearing a polka-dotted ascot suggested.

"Possibly." The head arana looked back to Evangeline. "Well, *I* certainly wouldn't do it."

Evangeline felt like she was losing her mind. "You'd do it if you were going to get eaten!"

Murmurs from the spectators echoed in the large room.

"Eaten?" the head arana said, raising her eyebrows. "My dear, who's trying to eat you?"

"I—I—" Evangeline stammered. Then she pointed at the warrior who had ordered her capture. "*She* said it!"

The head arana frowned. "Are you planning to eat this prisoner, Taranta Lily?" Several aranae laughed quietly.

The taranta's face reddened. "Of course not, Center!" She shot Evangeline a dangerous glare. "More lies!"

"Well, she said *death*," Evangeline said.

"She did say death," chimed in one of the other soldiers.

The head arana put two long, delicate fingers to her temple and closed her eyes. Evangeline's mother did the same thing when Evangeline asked too many questions.

"She *always* says death," said another soldier, quietly.

"And it always makes them talk!" Taranta Lily snapped.

Evangeline was getting more and more confused. She looked at the head arana. "Your Majesty—"

The head arana burst into laughter. "Your Majesty! I like that!"

Evangeline blinked. "You're not a . . . a spider queen?" she asked.

"I am a Center," the Center said patiently, but with a hard undertone, as though she were explaining for the thousandth time. "A mayor. I am the Center of the town of Dark Light." She gave Evangeline a pointed look. "And I am not a spider."

"No," Evangeline said, feeling embarrassed.

The Center steepled her twenty fingers. "Now. You claim you are not Princess Desdemona, and yet you wear her face and wield the power of the Winter Kingdom." She glanced at the shards of webbing now melting into gooey lumps all over the floor.

Evangeline nodded. "Yes." *The power of the Winter Kingdom.* Was that what the exploding icy-blood thing she just did was? She had *power* here? It . . . it sure felt like it.

"She's lying," Taranta Lily said, poking Evangeline with the tip of her long sword.

"I'm not lying," Evangeline said to the Center. "My friend Hortense needs help."

"Your friend Hortense doesn't exist," Taranta Lily barked.

"She does!" Evangeline said. "She—wait! Look." She pulled the little white orb out of her pocket and held it out. "She gave me this."

"That doesn't mean any—" Taranta Lily began, but stopped short when Evangeline passed her hand over the orb and it started to glow, just as Hortense had shown her. The warrior looked from the orb to Evangeline to the Center. "I don't understand."

The Center's face was grave. "I do," she said. "Whoever she may be, this human has been telling the truth about one thing: that one of our own people needs our help. And we have wasted far too much time with unfounded suspicions." She rose, and everyone around her stood with her. "Tarantae, to the mouth of the cave. Grab a physician on your way. Be ready for an ambush from Oak. Go."

In an instant, the great rainbow room was a flurry of activity. Evangeline couldn't help her goose bumps as the tall aranae scuttled into action.

"You. Human." The Center pointed. "Come with me."

Evangeline followed the Center and the other aranae back through the starlit village of Dark Light and into the cave tunnels. She had to run to keep up, but running was easy in the Winter Kingdom.

"She was shot with a crossbow," Evangeline called as she ran. "In the shoulder. Can you help her?"

"In all likelihood," the Center replied, her long black legs striding easily over the rocky ground, her gray-streaked braids rippling like waves behind her. "Aranae are resilient, and our physicians are quite used to injuries from Oaken crossbows. If the bolt did not pierce her heart, it should be a simple matter." Her voice darkened. "Provided we have not wasted too much time already."

When they reached the entrance and spilled out onto the rubbly ledge, Evangeline stopped in her tracks. From here, she could see out over the dark forest—or what would have been the dark forest. All the orbs she had seen hanging from branches were now lit up like hundreds of little moons bobbing in a sea of trees. Their soft light spread away from the cave in curves and lines, forming a great, glowing web shape in the night.

"It's beautiful," Evangeline murmured.

The Center nodded. The orb light was reflected by her brass-spike crown and large, luminous eyes. "Thank you," she said. "Now, show us—where is your friend?"

Evangeline peered out over the forest. It took her a moment, but she found the shimmering black line of the little stream that wound through the trees. "That stream," she said to the group of aranae soldiers, pointing. "Follow it to the far edge of the web. That's where she is."

The soldiers set off over the shale and hunks of quartz, but the Center put a hand on Evangeline's shoulder and kept her in place. "Don't worry, they will find their way," she said. "Now, come back to the village and let's get you something to eat, little sister."

"Sister?" Evangeline said.

The Center smiled. "Only aranae can persuade the orbs to glow. It's because they are part of us. You can light the orbs, therefore you are one of us."

"I am?" Evangeline slipped a hand into her pocket and ran her fingers over the silken surface of the orb. "I've never really been a part of anything before."

The Center gave her shoulder a squeeze and let go. "I have a feeling you're going to be part of all our lives here in the Winter Kingdom, in some way or another."

17

The movements of the Dark Light physician reminded Evangeline of baking shows she'd seen on TV, only instead of two arms whirling, grabbing, smoothing, and wielding dainty instruments with precision, it was four. She watched the healer with fascination until she was certain Hortense would be fine. Evangeline felt her own breath returning to normal as she watched her friend's calm inhale-exhale-inhale.

Then Evangeline insisted she had to depart for the village of Oak at once. Sir Paw-on-Stone would be waiting for her there, ready to send her through the Crystal Gate to Desdemona. When Evangeline closed her eyes, she could still see the word written in the frosty mirror: *Help*. She had to hope the arctic fox was right: that the locked gate and the Tree of Ancient Amethyst would protect her sister from King Vair's cold rage until they could return to Earth together.

But the Center was stern—a trip to Oak through the nighttime woods would be long and dangerous. Evangeline needed sleep, and would make faster time in the morning. So she and Hortense curled up in silken hammocks under the scattered stars that watched over Dark Light.

At dawn, they set off. Evangeline, Hortense, and Taranta Lily, the arana warrior, followed the bubbling stream all the way through aranae country until the woods became thinner and brighter. By mid-morning, they had reached the rutted road.

Taranta Lily stopped and pointed. "The village of Oak lies in that direction, Your High—Evangeline. And Hortense's village of Gnashing lies in the other, scarcely a day's walk."

Hortense's pale face grew even paler. "No!" she said. "I mean—I don't want to go home. I feel fine, really. I want to go with you, Evangeline. I want to help you save your sister. You shouldn't have to do it alone."

Taranta Lily gave Hortense a curious look, then turned to Evangeline. "You do inspire fierce loyalty in your friends, don't you?"

"I don't know," Evangeline said, pulling her new long hooded cloak around herself. "I've never had friends." Something gnawed at her mind as she looked at Hortense, who stood stiffly in the long brown dress the aranae had given her as a disguise, two thin arms snugged into each sleeve. There was hardly a trace of her injury from the day before; not even a wad of bandages puffed out the fabric of her dress thanks to the expert work of the Dark Light physician.

But Evangeline couldn't forget the way the ugly crossbow bolt had struck down her friend. Hortense had already been hurt because of Evangeline.

"You shouldn't come with me, Hortense," she forced herself to say. "It's too risky. Even with your disguise . . ." She didn't want to offend anyone, but shoving a long-sleeved dress on an arana wasn't going to fool anybody. Hortense's black crystal-ball eyes and long fangs were still in full view. But Evangeline dropped the subject. "As Taranta Lily said, your village is only a day away," she said.

"I'm not going home," Hortense said in a firm voice Evangeline had never heard. She didn't know what to say, and for a moment, they just looked at each other.

Then Taranta Lily spoke. "There is one more bit of help I can offer you." She passed two hands over each of the girls, human and arana. Evangeline thought for a moment she was trying to light them up like the orbs. But when she looked over at Hortense, her jaw dropped.

She must be Hortense, Evangeline told herself. There was still something Hortense-y about her. But her face and neck were now longer, like the people of Oak, with two knobby horns on her head. The fingers sticking out of her long brown sleeves still ended with eggshell nails, but her skin was smooth instead of being covered with short, coarse hair.

"Look at yourself, Evangeline," Hortense said.

Evangeline stared at her reflection in Taranta Lily's shiny armor. Sure enough, her own face was lengthened, her eyes were in the wrong place, and her horns were even knobbier than Hortense's.

"It won't last," Taranta Lily said. "A day at most."

"Amazing!" Evangeline said. "How did you do it?"

The taranta couldn't hide a small, proud smile. "It's just an old trick. We have used the art of disguise for many generations." Her expression sobered. "Be careful in Oak. You should never trust your life to magic."

Evangeline swallowed. "But why do the people of Oak hate the aranae so much?"

Taranta Lily's eyes flashed and Evangeline expected her to answer angrily. But after a moment, the warrior's expression softened. "Because great tragedy has befallen them," she said, "and they believe we are to blame. Anger makes people dangerous, but grief makes them more dangerous still. Just . . . try to take care of your business in Oak as quickly as possible. Today they blame us. Tomorrow, they may blame you."

"Thank you," Evangeline said. "Thank you for everything."

Taranta Lily nodded. "May you find your sister, Evangeline," she said, then turned to Hortense. "And may you find whatever it is you seek."

With that, the taranta turned back toward arana country and Evangeline and Hortense continued down the rutted road. It made

Evangeline nervous to take this route—even with her disguised face, she still wore the same corduroys and white sweater the Lord High Keeper's guards might recognize if her long cloak flapped open in the breeze—but they didn't meet a single other person on the road. When they began to see the first little houses and stone walls of Oak, they encountered a few villagers leaning against fences or carrying buckets, but nobody paid the two young travelers much attention.

"Sir Paw-on-Stone said he'd be at the tavern," Evangeline said.

"If I were the only Keeper left, I'd be very worried," Hortense said soberly.

When they reached the center of town, Evangeline began to get nervous. This was not a bustling town square but a muddy crossroads with a crumbling well at the center. The afternoon was misty and gray, with the occasional spatter of frigid raindrops pelting Evangeline's face in bursts. Unlike in Rime Village or the aranae town of Dark Light, nobody here in Oak was chatting with their neighbors or browsing the market for fun. A few stalls laden with wet brown vegetables were set up, but neither the shoppers nor the sellers seemed very excited about it.

In fact, the only things remotely interesting about the muddy village of Oak were Evangeline and Hortense themselves, two strangers making their way suspiciously through town.

Even with their Oaken faces, Evangeline knew she and Hortense stuck out. She tugged at the hem of her sweater. Hortense wore her brown shawl over her head like a grandma, her horns poking up underneath it. With her long bag slung over her back, she slouched to make sure her long dress dragged on the soggy ground and covered her extra pair of white shoes.

As Evangeline and Hortense crossed the drab little square, the villagers of Oak watched out of the corners of their eyes and from under the brims of their worn old hats. Evangeline was very familiar with how people looked at you when they didn't want you to know about it. She usually got those kinds of stares on her first day at school. Of course, by the second day, everyone usually realized how boring she really was and the stares would stop.

These were still first-day stares—only this wasn't Crestlake Middle School. Evangeline felt her skin prickling as they squelched past the well. Next to it stood a wooden signboard sheltered by a little roof. Dozens of papers had been tacked to it. At first, Evangeline couldn't make sense of them—pictures of faces, dates, directions to places in the forest. Then, under the drawing of a young Oaken man wearing a knit cap, she saw the word *Missing*.

They were all missing, all these people, and the signboard was full of what they had left behind—places and times, descriptions of clothing they had been wearing, and the memories of their faces.

"No wonder this town is on edge," Evangeline murmured. She caught a glimpse of a woman passing into an alley with a crossbow on her back and nearly stumbled. But on second look, the woman was only carrying a load of kindling. Still, Evangeline knew the only reason people weren't running them out of town right now was because of the disguises. What had Taranta Lily said? *It won't last. A day at most.* She looked at Hortense, who, under her magical disguise, wore the face of this town's bitter enemies—the aranae, who the people believed had been abducting their friends and loved ones.

They had to find Sir Paw-on-Stone, and fast. Not only would their disguises fade, but with Hortense getting shot, it had taken all night to get to Oak in the first place. If Sir Paw-on-Stone was right, King Vair would reach the Crystal Gate in less than three days. Evangeline had to get her sister out of there before then. A king who would dig to the very center of the world to become immortal wouldn't hesitate to turn anyone who might want his job into a Popsicle.

"Listen," Hortense said as they reached the row of gray thatched buildings on the other side of the square.

Evangeline listened. "Music!" The muffled, peppy sound of a flute and drum, mixed with the hum of voices, drifted over the village of Oak like ghosts. Evangeline turned her head this way and that. "It's coming from over there."

"We've found our tavern," Hortense said as they hurried past flaking doors and wilted window boxes. At the end of the row was a squat building with wide windows. Through a slender black door, songs, warm smells, and smoke spilled out into the street.

A battered sign over the door showed what looked like a load of kindling, tied together with a thin rope, like the one the woman in the alley had been carrying.

"I wouldn't mind a seat by the fire," Hortense said, rubbing her hands together.

They sidled through the black door into a room bathed in the yellow light of candles. Evangeline's boots stuck to the floor as they made their way deeper inside, winding around groups of hunched villagers nursing tall glasses. She expected the tavern to go silent when they entered, like in old Westerns, but the citizens of Oak seemed to have more important things to do than gawk at the newcomers. They studied Evangeline and Hortense with sly glances, but the two Oaken-looking strangers were not quite interesting enough to cause the tavern to screech to a halt. It's not like they were *aranae*.

In the corner, the flute and drum players were hooting and thumping away. Hortense took a couple of steps in their direction, smiling, but the handful of villagers gathered around them closed ranks and shut her out. Her shoulders slumped.

"I don't see Sir Paw-on-Stone," Evangeline whispered. "A white fox in a purple cape would definitely stick out here."

"Shall we ask the proprietor?" Hortense asked. She nodded toward the greasy bar, where a giraffe-like bartender with a potbelly and pink eye patch stood wiping a glass with a dirty rag. Although the tavern ceiling felt lofty to Evangeline, the bartender's pink, stick-up hair almost grazed it.

Evangeline scanned the tavern once more for Sir Paw-on-Stone. He had to be here by now. Maybe he'd rented a room. "Yeah," she said to Hortense. "Let's ask." They approached the bar.

"Welcome to the Bundle of Sticks," the bartender said, in a voice like the kids who were too cool to read aloud in class. "What do you want?"

Up close, he towered over Evangeline. She wasn't particularly short (as with most things in her life, she was average), but it seemed to her the Winter Kingdom was chock full of exceptionally tall people—the villagers of Oak, the aranae, and the menacing Lord High Keeper. Even Hortense could have reached up and brushed her fingers against the smoke-yellowed plaster of the tavern's high ceiling.

Evangeline leaned into the bar and motioned for the bartender to bend down. He rolled his eye. She cast a furtive look over her shoulder and motioned again. With a sigh, the bartender set his glass on the bartop and leaned down. "I'm meeting someone here," Evangeline whispered.

"Good for you," the bartender said in a bored voice.

"He's—he might be undercover," she went on. "In disguise."

"Uh-huh," the bartender said.

"Have you seen him?" Evangeline asked.

The bartender straightened up and made a vague gesture at the busy room. "I've seen all of *them*. Is your undercover friend one of them?"

Evangeline beckoned him again, and with an even bigger eye roll than before, the bartender leaned down. *"He's a fox,"* she whispered, then winked.

"What was that?" the bartender said. "Did you just wink?"

"I—yes," Evangeline said, a little embarrassed. "I was being secretive."

The bartender crossed his arms. "Is your friend a fox, or is he not really a fox?" he asked testily. "The wink makes it a bit unclear."

"He's a fox," Hortense piped up. "Probably wearing a purple cape with gold decorations."

The bartender lolled his good eye in Hortense's direction, but stiffened when he saw her. Evangeline tensed. Instead of seeming bored and a bit annoyed, the horse-faced bartender was now focused. His eye narrowed.

Evangeline remembered one gray February day in the kitchen with her mother. The curtains were closed tight, but all of a sudden, in the middle of breakfast, Mom had stopped chewing her toast. She sat there, frowning and frozen at the table, and then sniffed. "Snow," she'd said in a low voice. Sure enough, when Evangeline went out to catch the bus, it was snowing. Her mother had just *known*.

That was the look this bartender had now—the look on Evangeline's mother's face one second before she said *snow*. The bartender stared at Hortense with his narrowed eye, listening, sniffing, twitching his fingers . . .

He figured it out, Evangeline thought with a start. *He knows we don't belong here.*

Then she heard the tiniest squeak. She looked down to find a thin crust of ice had formed on the bartop where her hands rested.

Had she done that?

Quickly, she threw her elbows over the icy patch on the bar and leaned in. "So have you seen a fox around here or not?" she asked, no longer trying to be quiet. She just wanted the bartender to stop looking at Hortense.

It worked. The bartender blinked and turned back to Evangeline. He took a deep, irritated breath. "Yes. Your friend left last night."

Evangeline's elbows slipped and she almost face-planted on the bar. "Last *night*?"

"Yeah, last *night*," the bartender said, imitating her. "He was going to stay, but a couple guards from Bright Mine showed up and he hightailed it." He gave her a deadpan look. "I'm sure those events aren't related in the slightest."

Evangeline tipped her head back and squeezed her eyes closed. "Oh, *great*. What do I do now?"

The bartender started wiping down the bartop with his dirty rag. "Follow your heart."

Evangeline slouched against the bar. "Thanks, that's really inspiring."

"That's the *message*," the bartender said. "Your fox friend. He said if a young lady came looking for him, to tell her, 'Follow your heart.'"

"Oh," Evangeline said, perking up. "Oh!" Then she realized she had no idea what the message meant. ". . . Oh."

The bartender gave a shrug, then moved away, wiping the length of the bar with the rag.

"*Follow your heart,*" Hortense whispered. "What can it mean?"

Out of thin air, a little voice said, "Nothing."

"What?" Evangeline looked around. "Who said that?"

"The message means nothing," the voice of the invisible person whispered, "because it's not the message Sir Paw-on-Stone left. Don't trust the bartender. Don't trust *anyone here*."

18

Evangeline gripped the edge of the greasy bartop. "Are—are you a ghost?"

"No, I'm not a ghost," the disembodied voice squeaked. "I'm back here!"

Evangeline and Hortense leaned over the bar. On the other side, a girl with golden pigtails, large, square teeth, and long, upright rabbit ears stared up at them. She wore a dirty apron over a pink jumpsuit that matched her wide-apart eyes.

"Oh. Hey there," Evangeline said, but the girl only pursed her lips and looked nervously around.

"What are you doing?" called the bartender from the other end of the bar. "Get back to work!"

The pigtailed girl gave a frightened squeak and put her head down. She grabbed a tall glass and filled it with something from a dingy tap. "Here's your drink, miss," she said in a shaky voice, setting the glass down on a napkin and pushing it toward Evangeline.

"I didn't order—" Evangeline started, but with another nervous glance at the bartender, the girl hopped away and disappeared into the back room.

Evangeline and Hortense exchanged confused looks.

"What *is* this?" Evangeline said, picking up the glass. It was the color of watered-down orange juice, but there appeared to be little bits of fluff or vegetation or something floating in it.

"Look!" Hortense pointed to the napkin under the glass. Only it wasn't a napkin at all—it was a scrap of paper.

Evangeline slid it across the bartop toward her. "A note!" she whispered, then glanced around the busy tavern. *"Meet me in the alley,"* she read in a low voice before slipping it into her pocket.

Leaving the mystery beverage, Evangeline and Hortense made their way outside into the late afternoon. The village of Oak, nestled in a valley, was warmer than the forest that clung to the mountain, but the mud here was still tinged with ice. Hortense pulled her shawl tightly over her ears as they ducked into the alley next to the Bundle of Sticks.

Suddenly, a cry from the street made them stop in their tracks. Some kind of kerfuffle was going on in the town square. Cautiously, from the shadow of the alley, Evangeline and Hortense peeked around the edge of the building.

A small crowd had gathered by the well, and at its center stood three people. Two wore long red cloaks that cut through the grays and browns of Oak village as vibrantly as if they were traffic lights. The third, Evangeline felt sick to realize, was the Lord High Keeper himself. With one massive, icy hand, he gripped Evangeline's discarded mortal band. With the other, he held a small, knobby-horned man up by his neck. The man wore a simply embroidered cape made of brown velvet that flapped as he kicked his legs. A pretty brown hat lay in the mud beneath him where it must have fallen from his balding head.

"A white fox, an arana, and Princess Desdemona!" the Lord High Keeper bellowed. "Surely a trio like that would stick out in a soggy, disgusting village like this! We *know* they came thorough a portal nearby! *Where are they?*"

Evangeline and Hortense pressed themselves against the alley wall, utterly still. The Lord High Keeper's booming accusations reverberated off the bricks. "Don't lie to me, Mr. Mayor! *Three* dangerous fugitives under your nose, and you *haven't seen them*?" There was a wet *thud*, as though the Lord High Keeper had tossed his prisoner into the mud at his feet. Evangeline held her breath.

After what felt like an eternity, she could hear the normal sounds of a less-than-bustling town square begin to drift into the alleyway again. The Lord High Keeper and his red-cloaked assistants must have moved off. Evangeline unclenched her muscles. She risked a peek out into the square. A few people had helped the mayor to his feet.

A moment later, a door creaked open behind them and a small figure hurried out into the gloom. Evangeline and Hortense crept along the alley wall and met the pigtailed girl behind a pile of old wooden crates.

"You're in danger," the girl said, without even introducing herself.

"We know," Evangeline said, although she wasn't sure if the girl meant they were in danger from the Lord High Keeper or the mine guards or the citizens of Oak or the aranae or something else entirely. "Can you help us?"

"Do I *look* like I can help you?" the girl asked, wringing her hands. It seemed like she might burst into tears. "What am I supposed to do if that terrible Lord High Keeper comes back? I—I just don't know."

Truthfully, Evangeline couldn't imagine this long-eared, buck-toothed person going to battle against the formidable forces of the Winter Kingdom. But she said, "You've already helped us. You warned us about the bartender."

The girl brightened. "Yes!" she said. "I did. I did do that." Her ears twitched. "He can't catch me out here talking to you. I have to be fast."

"How did you know the bartender gave us a false message?" Hortense asked slowly.

The girl's eyes widened so much Evangeline could see the whites all around. "Because I *heard* him. The fox. I heard what he said. He didn't say 'follow your heart.' Nope."

A creak from the back door of the tavern made them all jump. The three of them pressed their backs against the wall of the alley and held their breath. But after a few moments, nothing happened.

"What did the fox say?" Evangeline asked.

The pigtailed girl closed her eyes, nodding, as though she were reliving the moment. "He said—"

Slam! The door to the tavern burst open. All of a sudden, the pink-haired, eye-patched bartender loomed in the shadows of the alleyway. "Polly!" he roared.

With a screech, the long-eared girl put her trembling hands to her face and started to cry. It sounded like a little balloon squeaking its air out.

The bartender thumped over to the pile of crates and folded his arms. "Stop that! It's annoying!" Polly's weeping intensified; her whole body shuddered.

Evangeline stepped forward. Hortense had said she was brave, so she might as well pretend. "Hey, leave her alone!" she said. *It might not be a good idea to draw attention to yourself*, she thought, too late.

The bartender scowled. "You! You might be almost as annoying as her. Get out of here."

"No," Evangeline said, sticking her chin out. "Not until you leave Polly alone."

"Leave her alone?" The bartender looked surprised. "Leave *her* alone? Kid, you don't understand—"

"I didn't do it!" Polly squealed. "I'm innocent! Please, sir! Don't send me to Bright Mine!"

"It's okay, Polly," Evangeline said, taking her hand.

"Oh, *sure*," the bartender spat. "Yeah. It's okay. Everything's fine." He jutted a finger in Polly's direction. "Except for my missing money!"

Polly's sad wails echoed off the alley walls. "I didn't steal anything!" she cried. "I promise! I love this job!"

"She says she didn't do it," Evangeline said, giving Polly's hand a squeeze.

"And I say I'm a beautiful fairy queen with wings of gold," the bartender said. "Get out of here, all of you. If I see any of your sorry butts in my tavern again, I'll send for the prison wagon!" With that, he stumped back into the Bundle of Sticks and slammed the door behind him.

Polly fell to her knees in a sad, adorable little heap. Evangeline crouched next to her on the icy dirt of the alley.

"What was the fox's message?" Hortense said, speaking for the first time since the bartender had burst from the door.

"Give her a minute," Evangeline said.

"N-no, I'm all right." Polly wiped her nose with the sleeve of her jumpsuit. She got to her feet and took a couple of deep breaths. "The *real* message your friend left for you was 'chase the stars.'"

Evangeline looked up. The gray sky was just beginning to think about darkening itself for evening. "'Chase the stars'? What does that mean?"

Polly's big eyes lit up. "I've been thinking about it, actually, and I have an idea. But we'll have to wait until nightfall."

"'We'?" Hortense snapped.

Polly's lower lip quivered. "I mean, if you don't want my help—I know I'm pretty useless—"

"Of course we want your help," Evangeline said, afraid Polly might start crying again. She gave Hortense a stern look. What was her problem?

Polly cleared her throat, collecting herself. "First, we've got to get you hidden," she said. "Your magic's starting to wear off."

Evangeline gave a start. "I—you know about that?" She looked over at Hortense. Sure enough, the faint suggestion of large black orbs were starting to show behind her giraffe-looking eyes. Hortense looked back at Evangeline with the same surprise.

"I've known all along," Polly said, pointing to her ears. "I can hear through magic." She looked fearfully at Hortense. "You're an *arana*, like the ones who have been taking our people." She turned to Evangeline, eyes shining. "And you're—you're a *princess*."

19

"I just—what does that even mean, *chase the stars*?" Hortense asked. She and Evangeline were seated on a bale of hay in the old barn Polly had led them to. They hadn't seen anyone on the road that led out of town deeper into the valley, but Polly stood guard by the gap in the wall planks, ears twitching. They waited. The sun had dipped below the tree line and the sky was almost dark.

Evangeline shrugged. "Polly has an idea, I guess."

"Yes, I know." Hortense's voice was flat. She folded her arms, two still snugged uncomfortably into each sleeve.

"Okay, what's wrong?" Evangeline asked. "You've been acting weird ever since Polly helped us at the tavern."

Hortense leaned in. "*Did* she help us? How do you know she's not working for the Lord High Keeper and the king?"

Evangeline stifled a laugh. "*Polly?* Are you kidding?" She glanced over to the other end of the long barn where the little rabbit-eared girl was peering intently into the evening. Polly twitched her head this way and that, blond pigtails shuddering. Suddenly, she gave a frightened squeak and froze like a squirrel. After a moment, she relaxed and continued her vigil.

"I mean—look at her!" Evangeline whispered. "She looks like she should be hopping around the garden, cowering from thunderstorms in the rosebush. She's probably one comforting hug away from singing us a song about friendship and cupcakes."

"She's certainly adorable," Hortense murmured. "Her and that fox."

"I don't know why you're suspicious of everyone," Evangeline said, slightly bitter. She studied her new friend's pale face and alien eyes in the shadows of the silent barn.

"They're coming!" a little voice chirped. Polly came bouncing toward them. "Princess Desdemona, they're coming! Through the woods! Oh dear, oh dear!"

Evangeline and Hortense jumped to their feet. "Who's coming?" Evangeline asked in a hushed voice. "Should we hide?"

"Yes!" Polly cried, hiding her eyes. "That is—that is, no!" She was shivering.

"Yes or no?" Hortense hissed.

Polly peeked out from behind her hands. "It's the Night Gambol! They're almost here."

"The Night Gambol?" Hortense seemed to relax. "The fairies? You're afraid of the *fairies*?"

"No!" Polly squeaked. "I mean—no! A little." She held up a thumb and forefinger very close together. "Just this much."

"Fairies?" Evangeline said. "For real?"

"Come see," Polly whispered, beckoning. The three of them crept through the empty barn, which still smelled like horses and sweet grass. At a biggish gap in the planks, Polly pointed.

Evangeline peered into the darkness. At first, she couldn't see anything but the deserted road and the gloomy trees on the other side. But then there was a flash, just a pinprick of white light. As she watched, it grew bigger and closer. Then there were more, blinking into the night, forming a twinkling procession that wound through the woods, closer and closer.

Polly tugged at Evangeline's sweater. "Get down!" They ducked back behind the barn wall as the little white lights began to pass within arm's reach. Up close, Evangeline could see that the procession was made up of dozens of small, winged people—fairies! They skipped and twirled as they made their way through the night, laughing with voices like tiny bells. And each fairy cradled something glowing in their arms. In only a few moments, the whole group had gone by and was flickering back into the forest.

Evangeline stared. "They look like . . ."

"Stars," Hortense whispered.

Polly gave a little hop. "*Chase the stars*. Like your message from that fox."

"Where are they going?" Evangeline asked.

Polly shrugged. "I don't know where they go. But I watch them pass by this barn. They're so beautiful. I . . . Sometimes I come here to sleep when—when I can't stay at the Bundle of Sticks." Her face fell and she cast her big eyes downward. "I often do stupid things, you know, drop a glass or lose a coin . . . then the bartender gets mad at me . . ." She bit her bottom lip with her large, square teeth.

Evangeline looked from Polly's sad face to the cold, empty barn. What would she do now that she couldn't go back to her job in Oak? "You could come with us," Evangeline ventured. "Our journey might be more dangerous than the Bundle of Sticks, but at least you'll be with friends."

A wide grin slowly spread across Polly's face. "Friends?" she said, her voice quivering.

"Not to ruin the moment," Hortense said, "but if we're going to chase the stars, we need to do it now."

"Oh!" Polly exclaimed. "Yes!" She looked at Evangeline. "Do you think my idea's right? Is that what the message means?"

Evangeline watched as the last of the fairy lights threaded their way deeper into the forest. "It's as good a clue as any. What do you think, Hortense?"

Hortense shrugged. "Let's go."

They slipped through the gap in the boards and tiptoed across the deserted road into the trees on the other side, keeping the lights in sight but well in the distance. After a few minutes, the forest thinned and they found themselves creeping across a vast field littered with boulders and squat, dark bushes. The ground was still hard and cold, but there was no snow here. Some of the bushes even sported flowers. It was too dark for Evangeline to tell what color the flowers were, but they were big and bright.

Suddenly, Polly screeched.

Evangeline jumped behind a bush. "What? What?"

"I'm sorry!" Polly said, turning her face away. "It's just . . ." She pointed backward. "I'm sorry." She took a deep breath. "I'm okay. I'm sorry. I just wasn't expecting it."

Evangeline turned around and saw Hortense behind them. The taranta's magic had worn off. Hortense stood now as she really was, long fangs and all. And as Polly cowered, trying to regain control of her breathing, Hortense's huge black eyes began to shine with tears.

"Oh, Harriet, I'm so sorry," Polly whimpered.

"Hortense," Hortense said, which made Polly whimper more.

"Hortense! I'm sorry!" She sniffed loudly. "I can't do anything right! I'm a bad friend."

"You're not a bad friend," Hortense murmured. "Maybe we should—"

Polly backed into a flowering bush, wrapping the branches around herself protectively. "It's just that you—not *you*—but, you know, the *spiders* have been taking people from Oak, and I wasn't ready to see you like that, like in my nightmares . . ."

"I'm not a spider," Hortense whispered.

"Come on," Evangeline said. "We're losing the lights." The fairies were so far ahead, they seemed to have missed Polly's outburst entirely. And they were disappearing fast.

Evangeline felt a hand on her arm.

"I . . . ," Hortense said, then closed her mouth. Then she looked at Polly, and back to Evangeline. "Since the magic has worn off, I think it might be better if I stay."

"Stay?" Polly asked. "What do you mean?"

Hortense sat on a rock and slipped her bag off her shoulders. "I can find my own way from here," she said quietly. "I don't think I should come with you anymore, Evangeline. It's better if you don't travel with me."

Polly gasped. "That is *so brave* of you, Hortense. You are truly an amazing friend." She took Evangeline's hand and tugged. "Let's go."

Evangeline felt like she'd just been kicked in the stomach by an ice troll. "Hortense, no! What are you talking about?"

Hortense looked down. "You said yourself I shouldn't come, after Dark Light. You were right. What if Sir Paw-on-Stone is with the Night Gambol? Do you know what fairies do when they see an arana?" She blinked as Evangeline was silent. "They scream and run away."

Polly nodded. "They do. They do scream and run away."

Hortense pulled her brown shawl off her head and wrapped it around her shoulders. "Please go. Your sister needs you. It's going to be dangerous enough. You don't need to be traveling with an arana."

Polly tilted her head at Evangeline. "Your sister?" she asked.

"I'll explain later," Evangeline said.

"Of course," Polly said. "Now, we have to go or we'll lose them altogether!" She gave Evangeline's hand another tug, and Evangeline took a few reluctant steps.

"Go!" Hortense snapped.

Evangeline saw the last fairy light blink away across the field. She had to go now. But it didn't feel right. "I'll send a message to you after I find my sister," she said. Her voice wobbled.

Hortense gave a half-hearted nod. "Goodbye."

And with Polly pulling her along, Evangeline left Hortense in the shadows of the flowering shrubs and hurried after the twinkling lights of the Night Gambol.

She was surprised by how fast Polly sprinted across the boulder-strewn field. She was almost as fast as Evangeline herself, except when the terrain opened up and Evangeline could really *run*. They bounded through the night, eyes fixed on the spot in the distance where the fairy lights had disappeared.

Eventually they came to a high, rocky pass. Evangeline slowed to a walk, watching, listening. The steep slopes of the pass on either side seemed to press in on her, blocking out the sky, making the nighttime even darker than it should have been. Her footsteps on the gravel felt too loud.

"Come on!" Polly hop-skipped ahead. "I think they went into the forest at the other side of this pass!"

"Be careful," Evangeline said. "I don't like it here."

"Then hurry up!" Polly called.

Carefully, Evangeline followed her through the passageway, which grew narrower and narrower. Polly seemed more at ease now than she'd been in the barn. Her ears weren't twitching at all. That was a good sign; there was probably nothing to worry about. Slowly, Evangeline kept walking, her feet crunching the ground. *Crunch . . . crunch . . . crunch . . . crack!*

With a lurch, Evangeline felt herself flung forward. The ground gave way with a snap and a swish, and then the night air was rushing by, pulling her hair skyward as her body dropped.

Thump. Evangeline hit solid darkness feet first and folded. She groaned and rolled onto her side.

"Princess? Princess?" a little voice called from above.

Evangeline sat up. "Polly! I'm down here!" She put her arms out and found a rough dirt wall. "I'm okay, but I think I fell into a pit or something!" She peered up. There was nighttime sky above her.

A head poked into view, two long ears silhouetted against the sky. "Your Highness?"

"Polly!" Evangeline called. She felt her way along the dirt wall. No openings. No corners. And no rope. She knew there were only rocks and scrubby bushes on the surface. But she had an idea. "You've got to get Hortense!" she yelled up at Polly. "She can't have gone far. I think she could get me out of here with her silk!"

"I think you're right! The arana could definitely get you out of there!" Polly yelled back. Her long ears twitched. Then her squeaky voice darkened. "That's why I made sure she didn't come with us."

20

"What?" Evangeline fell back against the wall of the pit. "What do you mean?"

Polly was still watching from above, but Evangeline couldn't see her expression in the darkness, only the outline of her head. "I told you I can hear through magic," Polly said, pointing to her long ears. "But that's not all I can hear. Not even close."

Evangeline was still reeling. What was going on? "I don't understand," she said.

Polly gave a laugh. "At first, I wasn't sure I'd be able to catch you. Not with your arana friend hanging around. But then I heard Hortense's doubts. Could you, a princess, really want to be friends with *her*? I heard your doubts, too. You didn't quite trust her, the ugly spider. Not her, not the grumpy, one-eyed bartender. Not the way you immediately trusted cute little me."

Evangeline's stomach twisted. She felt sick. It was true.

"Oh, yes, I heard your doubts," Polly said. "And I *fed them*. I used them to get rid of the arana. She could have helped you escape my trap! I had to get you here alone." She leaned farther over the edge of the pit. "Now, what's this nonsense about a sister?"

"I'm not telling you anything," Evangeline snapped.

Polly shrugged. "It doesn't matter. You'll tell the Lord High Keeper what he wants to know. He's on his way. But it's going to be a long night. They don't usually get here until morning, when I'm long gone."

Evangeline frowned. "They don't usually—what do you mean?"

Polly laughed. She spoke in a high, mocking voice. *"Please, sir! You've got to help me! The aranae from the cliff have taken my friend! Follow me—I'll show you where!"*

"You!" Evangeline steadied herself against the dirt wall. "You've been luring people from Oak into this trap! It wasn't the aranae at all! Why—why would you do that?"

"You don't think it's clever?" Polly said. "The king demands more workers for Bright Mine every day. The Lord High Keeper has been very grateful for my secret little supply from Oak. He gives me a generous finder's fee."

Evangeline pounded on the wall. "That's why you didn't betray us in the village. If the villagers knew about you—if the *aranae* knew—"

"But they don't, princess," Polly said. "They don't." She waved. "Well, toodle-oo, new friend. It's been fun! But I've got to go." And with that, she hopped out of sight.

The pit was silent except for a gentle breeze touching the ground high above. Evangeline pressed her hands to the wall, feeling up and down, making her way all around the edge. There was nothing to grab on to, no roots or handy jutting rocks. She could scrape the dirt away with her fingernails if she worked at it, but there was no way she could carve enough footholds to climb out before morning. After a few minutes, she just slid down the wall and sat, in the dirt and the darkness, feeling sorry for herself.

She remembered Hortense's orb in her pocket. *Well, at least I don't have to sit in the dark*, she thought, pulling it out and passing her hand over it. The little orb shone moon-blue, casting shadows and startling a few bugs, who went scuttling back into their holes.

The light gleamed off something small next to Evangeline on the ground. Curious, she picked it up.

"Oh no," she whispered.

It was a small button that said JELLY BEAN HUGS. The last time she'd seen that button, it had been pinned to Sir Paw-on-Stone's purple cape.

Evangeline's heart sank. The white fox had fallen into Polly's trap, and that double-crossing bunny girl had probably already handed him over to the Lord High Keeper himself. Sir Paw-on-Stone had taken a risk helping Evangeline escape, and he'd been captured. Who knew what would happen to him now?

And it was all Evangeline's fault.

Her eyes became hot with regret. Her mother had been right all along. Why had Evangeline come to the Winter Kingdom? The only things she'd accomplished so far were being thrown in a prison wagon, captured by aranae, and tricked into falling into a pit.

The only smart thing she'd done was make friends with Hortense, and look how that had turned out. With just a little suggestion from Polly, she'd left Hortense alone in the middle of nowhere. *I'm a terrible friend*, she thought.

On top of it all, Sir Paw-on-Stone was the only one in all of the Winter Kingdom who could send Evangeline through the Crystal Gate to the Tree of Ancient Amethyst and her sister. Without him, there was no way she could reach Desdemona in time to save her from King Vair. She was going to lose her sister before she even found her. What on earth had made Evangeline think she could rescue an actual *princess*? She was in way over her head, and it wasn't just this stupid pit.

She turned the silky orb around in her hands, watching the shadows on the dirt wall change as the light moved. Then a little thought, more like an itch at the very edge of her brain, began to peep.

You are a princess, too, Evangeline.

Evangeline took a deep breath. "Pbbbbt!" She blew a raspberry. That was what she did when she wanted to block out thoughts she didn't want to think. A princess! Her!

But . . .

She let herself think it just a little bit. *It's true, isn't it? It has to be true.* But what did it mean? She thought about her mother's secret ice-blue gown, imagining the feel of its heavy beading, its scent of snow. She thought about the photograph in the fairy forest, and the look of serenity and *confidence* on her mother's face as she played the violin. Was that her *real* mother? Were the boring houses and drawn curtains and bland clothes only an elaborate costume? She thought about Mom's calm lake expression. Was it hiding a *queen*?

And, Evangeline asked herself, *what kind of queen is she?*

Evangeline had to get to Desdemona, and to do it, she needed Sir Paw-on-Stone. But how?

"The first step," she said aloud, "is to get out of this pit." She got to her feet and looked around. "I can't climb up. There's nothing here to make a rope out of. There's nobody to help me up above." She put the glowing orb back in her pocket, jutted her chin, and straightened her spine. "But I am a princess of the Winter Kingdom. This is *my* land, and no silly pit is going to keep me from my sister."

Then, suddenly, she felt that minty-blood feeling, as though jets of ice were snaking in through her pores, electrifying her. She remembered the ice that had formed under her fingers on the bartop in Oak, the wonderful *crack* of the spider silk snap-freezing around her in Dark Light. She remembered the snow on Earth that seemed to follow her—*No*, she realized. *It didn't follow me, did it? It answered me. Because I called it. Every time, it was me. I called the snow, and it came.*

She had always loved the snow. And now she knew that the snow had always loved her. But winter in the suburbs was pale and flat compared to the beautiful ferocity of the Winter Kingdom. Evangeline gazed into the night sky far above her. This valley might be dry and flowering, but the snow-blanketed mountains watched from all sides, bright and alive and prickling with ice. Evangeline could *feel* them. The winter here was strong. And it was hers.

"Out of this pit!" she called, in a commanding tone that didn't sound a bit like her own. It didn't sound like the Queen of Hearts, either. It was real. *Was that me?* she wondered. It felt like her mouth talking, like the air from her own lungs. But her voice was different. It vibrated the tiny crystals of ice that clung to the rocks around her. "I need to go *up!*" She flung her arms out in front of her.

The snow came.

It bubbled up from the depths of the pit, rumbling like a thousand purring cats. It gathered at Evangeline's feet, swirling out like glitter from her hands and forming, peeling, tumbling from the dirt walls.

Evangeline rose. The snow beneath her carried her up, *up*. She looked skyward, her hair flying back from her face, and laughed. Soon, the whole pit was filled with pristine snow. Then it stopped.

Evangeline took a few graceful steps back onto the ground of the narrow pass. Her fingers tingled, her boots sparkled with flakes of ice, and her hair seemed still to be flying, even in the quiet air.

"Sit tight, sister," she said in her new, powerful voice. *"I'm coming."*

21

Evangeline sat on a rock high above the pit at the edge of the narrow pass. She bit into what she really hoped was an apple. It was lavender with yellow spots, which was unusual for an apple, she had to admit, but she had stolen it out of what was most definitely an orchard—rows and rows of healthy trees covered in fat fruits. There were even a few baskets lying around, and one stout branch had a ladder leaning against it.

"I mean, it *has* to be some kind of apple, right?" she said, only it sounded more like mud and spit since she was chewing the maybe-apple while she spoke. "There's, like, *no* chance it's deadly poison." She chewed some more. "Hardly any chance."

The maybe-apple was sweet and stringy, like a squash crossed with a strawberry. Evangeline felt bad about taking it without per-mission, but she hadn't had anything to eat since yesterday, and the trees were so burdened with fruit it was just dropping onto the ground. Besides, it was important to mount rescue missions on a full stomach.

To save her sister, she needed to get through the Crystal Gate. For that, she needed Sir Paw-on-Stone. And to get to Sir Paw-on-Stone, she needed the Lord High Keeper, who, if Polly had been telling the truth, would be here soon to pick up whatever new prisoners might have fallen into her trap.

Polly. Evangeline took an angry bite of maybe-apple. She would deal with Polly later. For now, she just had to wait for the Lord High Keeper. Once he passed by, she would creep down the rocky embankment and follow him. Hopefully, he would lead her to wherever Sir Paw-on-Stone was being held.

After a few more generous bites of fruit, Evangeline's hunger stopped twisting her guts around, and she was able to focus. "If Polly's message was fake," she said aloud, getting used to her new Princess Voice, "then the bartender's must have been real." She turned the lavender fruit over and traced a design over its spots. "'Follow your heart.'"

Evangeline sat for a moment trying to feel her own heart beating in her chest. It was there, a subtle rhythm keeping her alive, but it didn't seem to be leading her in any particular direction. What could Sir Paw-on-Stone have meant? If only she had more time! *Two days,* she realized, until King Vair would reach the Crystal Gate and destroy the white fox's magical lock with the rootball stone. Only two!

Not that Sir Paw-on-Stone's message mattered now. He hadn't counted on falling into Polly's trap. Evangeline finished the maybe-apple down to its stringy core and flung it into a bush.

While she waited for the Lord High Keeper to appear on the road below, Evangeline swept off a flat part of the rock. Concentrating hard, thinking about delicate ice over a still pond, she touched the rock. A film of ice began to form, smooth and clear.

Evangeline peered into the ice, dreading what she might see. Dreading that it had already been too long and the king and his soldiers had found her sister at last.

"Desdemona," she called. "Are you there?" Ripples of color shuddered the thin layer of ice, blurry and wriggling. After a moment, Evangeline saw her sister, surrounded by purple, sitting cross-legged on the ground. She had something in her hands . . . a book! She was reading a book. Such an ordinary activity. What kinds of books did Princess Desdemona like? Did she have the same taste as Evangeline?

Evangeline couldn't hold on, and a moment later, the image was gone and the veneer of ice on the flat rock cracked and melted away.

But she had seen enough. Her sister was still hidden, still safe! With a burst of energy and laughter, Evangeline flung her left arm out in front of her in an arc. Where she traced the air, a glittering rainbow of snowflakes drifted down, catching the morning light. She threw both arms out and spun around, still laughing as a mini winter whirlwind surrounded her.

Voices floating up from below startled her. Quickly, she ducked behind the rock and peeked out.

Two men in long red cloaks and wide hats came into view, trudging down the road: the Lord High Keeper's helpers. *He's not with them,* Evangeline was disappointed to realize. The red-cloaked men flanked a tall cage on wheels, which was being pulled by a sad-looking donkey. Inside the wheeled cage below were a handful of people, hunched and downcast.

"Hurry up!" one of the Red Cloaks barked. His reedy voice carried all the way up the slope. "We'll never reach Bright Mine by nightfall at this rate!"

"My cousin went to Bright Mine and a year later they gave us his bones in a sack!" one of the people in the cage said, wailing.

"Please," another cried out, "take us to prison instead!"

"Quiet!" the Red Cloak snapped. "Nobody's going to prison. It's Bright Mine for all of you, so get used to it!"

Evangeline remembered the haunted looks of the miners, and the way they trudged through the courtyard with their heavy wagons. She remembered what Hortense said: *It's a terrible place. And once you go in, you never come out.*

Was that going to be the fate of these people in the cage, thrown to the mines? Evangeline felt her jaw clench. Her fingers and toes twitched, like icy caterpillars trying to turn into butterflies. She itched to call her snow down on the Red Cloaks.

Isn't that a little complicated for you, dear? her mother's voice said in her head.

"No," Evangeline whispered. She squeezed her eyes shut.

Why don't you leave that sort of thing for the other kids? came her mother's voice again.

Evangeline opened her eyes. The procession of guards and prisoners was moving swiftly, heading into the pass where they would be sheltered by the high rock sides. Evangeline watched helplessly. *Why can't I help them?* she scolded herself. Then she wondered, *Why didn't I have any idea I had these powers in the first place?*

And she thought of her mother, and all her little comments. All the ways she had covered up Evangeline's true identity. No sports, because Evangeline was too slow and uncoordinated—or *was* she? No clubs, because Evangeline wouldn't make friends easily—or *would* she have? No birthdays, no fun clothes, no *anything*. And the whole time, Evangeline's own sister was here in the Winter Kingdom—a princess!

"It wasn't because I was painfully ordinary," Evangeline said. "It was because I *wasn't*." She stood up.

"Come, snow," she whispered, raising her arms. "Come, winter. I need your help." The tips of her fingers and toes started to buzz. The air swirled around her.

Then *swish! Whoosh! Roar!* Evangeline's loyal snow jumped forth from the dry earth and fell in sheets from the sky. It raced like a tidal wave down the slope of the embankment, straight toward the Red Cloaks.

They heard it before they saw it, pausing and turning their heads with nearly identical, curious expressions. Then their faces twisted in horror as they saw the mass of white barreling toward them. They ran.

Swoop! Evangeline threw her arms to one side, dragging the torrent of snow away from the cage on wheels and the amazed donkey, toward the fleeing Red Cloaks. It was upon them in seconds, knocking them off their feet and carrying them along, head over heels over head, until they both tumbled into Polly's dreadful pit. Then, from her perch atop the hill, she turned to the cage on wheels on the road below.

Concentrating harder than she'd ever done, she took a deep breath and *blew*. She stared at the metal door of the cage, focusing on it, narrowing her airstream. She followed the outline of the door, then traced the length of the donkey's harness. The astonished prisoners inside drew away from the door, huddling at the back of the cage. Then, with a bright *crack!*, the bars of the door, as well as the harness, froze solid and crumbled. The prisoners cried out and hugged one another, leaping from the cage. They turned to the embankment, searching for their rescuer, but Evangeline quickly hopped away from the edge and was hidden by the land.

"Woo-hoo!" she cheered, then blew a raspberry in the direction of the Red Cloaks in the pit.

Was it magic? She wasn't sure. It felt more real than that, a relationship, like a conversation with winter itself. But wherever her powers came from, she was learning to control them.

A rush of power surged through her blood vessels. "How overdramatic am I *now*, Mother?" she laughed, shooting a jet of ice from her fingertips at a nearby tree, where it splintered like glass into the branches. "Is *this* just me looking for attention?" *Crash!* Another, angrier jet of ice smashed against a boulder. "I had this power all along and you never told me!" *Smash! Crack! Shatter!*

"Please, stop!" came a terrified voice.

Evangeline froze, mortified. She looked around. Shards of ice lay everywhere, melting on the ground, sticking out of the trees like porcupine quills. But she couldn't find the person who had spoken.

"Um . . . if you're done having your fit," buzzed a muffled little voice, "maybe you could help me?"

"Help you?" Evangeline said cautiously. "Where are you?"

"I'm, uh, under a basket," the voice said, sounding hopeful.

Evangeline scanned the edge of the orchard. There were a few baskets strewn around. One nearby was overturned on a bare patch of ground. She went over to it and crouched down.

"In here?" she said, knocking on the side of the basket like a door.

"Yes! Yes!" the voice said, very hopeful now. "Flip it over and let me out!"

Evangeline hesitated. "How do I know you won't turn me in to the Lord High Keeper?"

"The—the Lord High Keeper?" the voice said worriedly. "Are you a criminal?"

Evangeline pulled her head back, offended. "No!"

"Then why would I turn you in to the Lord High Keeper?" the voice asked.

"Well, I don't know," Evangeline said. "Besides, what if you're dangerous? Are you going to attack me?"

"*Attack* you?" the voice said. "From the sound of things, you've been playing with whirlwinds and avalanches. Meanwhile, I'm stuck under a basket that was propped up with a stick! How dangerous do you think I am?"

"I don't know," Evangeline said. "I'm still getting used to the Winter Kingdom."

"Look," the voice said, weary now. "If you don't trust me, if you don't want to help me, then don't. I just . . . it's pretty dark in here and I'm awfully hungry. Could you at least slip an apple underneath?"

"Ha! They *are* apples!" Evangeline said. Then she bit her lip, thinking about the voice's words. *What am I doing?* she thought. *Am I really not going to help a sad little voice under a basket just because Polly betrayed me?* "I'm sorry," she said. "Of course I'll let you out."

She flipped up the basket. For a split second, there seemed to be nothing but a confusion of colors and movement underneath. "Thank you, thank you, thank you!" came a voice, tiny and shimmering like a gem. Something buzzed by her head.

"Arck!" Evangeline squeaked, startled. She turned this way and that but couldn't find whatever had flown from the basket. "Are you a bug?"

The voice sounded just at her left ear. "No!"

Evangeline twisted her neck. Something blurry that shimmered like the rainbow of light through a prism hovered so close to her nose she couldn't focus on it. She blinked as the whisper of a breeze, as if from hummingbird's busy wings, touched her cheeks and eyes.

"Can you—back up?" she asked.

"Oh, whoops!" the shiny little voice said. "Sorry." The blur moved away and Evangeline was finally able to get a good look at it. After everything she'd seen in the Winter Kingdom, she wouldn't have been at all surprised to meet a talking hummingbird. But this was no bird— it was a person, no taller than a banana, with sparkling blue skin, two short, curly horns, and long, swirling violet hair. He wore a tunic of woven pine needles, and he floated a couple of feet away, his shimmering wings beating so furiously they looked like a multicolored cloud around him.

"That's better," Evangeline said. She took a breath. "My name's Evangeline." This whole "introducing herself" thing was getting easier. Then, with a spark of pride, she added, "I'm a princess."

"Wow!" the flying person said, bobbing a little bow. "Sparrow Fall. Nice to meet you, Princess Evangeline. So nice. So nice to be rescued from that trap." His eyes were wide. "I think it was meant for lizards. Lizards love to steal apples."

Evangeline wasn't sure how you were supposed to greet a small blue person with rainbow wings, so she nodded. "Sparrow Fall. That's an interesting name."

"Is it?" Sparrow Fall buzzed upward in a diagonal, then back again. It reminded Evangeline of the way some people moved their eyes when they were thinking. "It's all right, I guess. Not as good as my brother Bear Attack. *Bear Attack!* Nice to meet you! *Roar!*"

"Bear Attack?" Evangeline sat back, palms on the warming ground. "Why would anyone be named Bear Attack?"

Sparrow Fall buzzed right, then left. "Um, in case you couldn't tell, I'm a fairy."

Evangeline looked at his tiny stature, glimmering wings, and pine-needle tunic. Even if she hadn't gotten a glimpse of the Night Gambol, she would have recognized him right away. He could have popped straight out of a picture book. "Yeah, I could, actually, tell," she said. "At least, I figured you weren't an ice troll."

"Oh, *thanks*." Sparrow Fall zipped over and under in a loop-the-loop. "Anyway, fairies are named after important things that happen the day they're born. A fledgling sparrow jumped from the nest just after I hatched. Hence, Sparrow Fall."

"And Bear Attack."

"Yep." Sparrow Fall bobbed up and down like a shrug. "Could be worse, I guess. I've got a cousin named Nothing."

Evangeline laughed. But it ended quickly. "Look, it's nice to meet you, and I'd love to chat, but I'm afraid something terrible has happened to my friend. He was supposed to meet me in Oak, and I thought maybe he'd be in that cage, but now—" She wasn't sure how to continue. She got to her feet, dusting granules of rock from her corduroys and the sleeves of her sweater.

"He's in trouble and you're going to save him," Sparrow Fall said. "Let me help!"

Evangeline studied her new fairy acquaintance. His chest was thrust out with importance, but his face seemed young. If he were a human, she would have thought he was probably around fifteen or sixteen; Hortense's age. She wanted to ask him, *How could you possibly help?* But it felt like something her mother would ask, so instead she said, "Why would you want to help me?"

Sparrow Fall alighted on a sand-colored rock. Now that his wings were still, Evangeline could really see them, wide and almost invisible, casting rainbows when the light hit them just right. "Well, first of all, I owe you for rescuing me," the fairy said.

"It's really okay," Evangeline said. "It was just a basket."

Sparrow Fall looked downcast. "It was just a basket to you," he said, "but I might have starved in there. It's a little embarrassing."

"I'm sorry," Evangeline said. *There I go, hurting people's feelings again,* she thought. Making friends was harder than it seemed—if that's what this was.

"No matter," the fairy said. "Anyway, second of all, I'm on my Crossing." When Evangeline tilted her head, curious, he went on. "When we, you know, come of age. We go out into the world and do something brave. My brother Bear Attack singlehandedly drove off the bears who were harassing our village." He paused, tapping his ankles against the branch. "Do humans do anything like that?"

"Some do," Evangeline said. "Not usually with bears."

The fairy zipped into the air again, hovering in front of Evangeline's face, his pointed chin held high. "I want to prove I'm just as brave as Bear Attack," he said.

"Listen," Evangeline said. "You're really nice to want to help me, but I'm going up against some dangerous people. Maybe even the Lord High Keeper himself. I think he might have taken my friend to Bright Mine, where the criminals go."

"Bright Mine!" exclaimed the fairy.

"Yeah." Evangeline felt her own resolve being tested as she talked about it. "But I have to rescue him. He's the only person who can help me get to the Tree of Ancient Amethyst." She breathed in. "And my sister."

Sparrow Fall dipped close to the grass, the way someone might lower their eyes as they were considering something. "The Tree of Ancient Amethyst? So your friend is a Keeper of the Crystal Gate?"

"Yes. Sir Paw-on-Stone. He's a white fox."

"A white fox!" Now the fairy zoomed up, almost smacking Evangeline in the face with his wide wings. "I know where your friend is!" he said excitedly.

Evangeline took a step back from the gusts of air from Sparrow Fall's flapping. "You saw him?"

"Yes, last night," the fairy said. "At least, I think it was him. I was prowling the outskirts of Glacier City. It's kind of a rough place. I thought I could do something brave, like stop a robbery or sing a song by myself in front of a lot of people."

"Uh-huh," Evangeline said, trying to imagine this delicate little person doing either of those things. *Do you have to be strong to be brave?* she wondered.

"Anyway," Sparrow Fall went on, "I was hanging around a tavern called the—the Jumping Frog? The Leaping Frog? The Sassy Toad? I don't remember. But I went in through the back door and there was this gross alley back there with all these rotting cabbages and I saw a white fox in a cage being guarded by some very hard, pointy people. The fox was wearing a purple cape and he had a strange collar on—it looked like it was made of emeralds."

"Sir Paw-on-Stone!" Evangeline cried. "Oh no!" It hurt her chest to think of her friend being held captive in a dirty alley, all because of her. "It must have been him," she said. "And they've got him in a mortal band."

Sparrow Fall's face became serious and he ducked his head, his curly little golden horns glinting in the sunlight. "Oh dear! Not a mortal band!"

Evangeline still wasn't entirely sure what mortal bands were. They were certainly heavy to wear. "Is that bad?" she asked.

Now the fairy looked at Evangeline with shock. "Of course it's bad! It dampens magic! To put a mortal band on a Keeper of the Crystal Gate, well—well, the whole kingdom would be at risk!"

"Dampens magic," Evangeline said. "That makes sense. They'd have to get rid of his magic in order to hold him. But he needs magic to unlock the Crystal Gate and get me through." *If only Hortense were here*, she thought with a pang of sadness. *She knows how to remove mortal bands.* She put her hands on her hips. "I'll just have to get that emerald necklace off him, then, when I rescue him. Somehow."

"*We'll* have to," said Sparrow Fall bravely.

Evangeline looked at him. He would fit in her pocket. He'd lost a battle with a basket on a stick. But he looked back at her with so much heart, she couldn't say no. "Very well. We'll go to Bright Mine together."

Sparrow Fall grinned. Then he said, "Oh, no! Not the mine. They didn't take your fox friend to the mine."

Evangeline's mouth opened in surprise. "They didn't?"

"No!" The fairy zipped from left to right, and right to left. "They took him to the dungeons of Glacier City Keep!" He shivered. "I know because those guys in the red cloaks were in the tavern singing a song about it. 'The dungeons! The dungeons! We'll hang you by your toes! And stick you with sharp objects!'" He frowned. "It's not much of a song, is it?"

"Maybe you can use your magic powers to help him escape," Evangeline said, thinking about stealthily breaking into a dank, well-guarded dungeon with a talkative, glittering, buzzing, rainbow-throwing fairy.

Sparrow Fall laughed. "Me? Magic powers?"

Evangeline blinked. "I just—you look pretty magical."

"This is *all* physics, baby," the fairy said, fluttering his wings. "But I think I know someone in Glacier City who might be able to help."

"Okay." Evangeline dusted off her long cloak. "Then let's go to Glacier City."

"Right," Sparrow Fall said. "Just—it's probably fine. Probably nobody will recognize you. It's not like a princess would ever set foot in a place like that."

"Great," Evangeline said, pulling her hood over her hair. Even though the magic snow of the Winter Kingdom seemed to be flowing through her veins, giving her strength, she wasn't thinking *great*. She was thinking, *What in the world have we gotten into?*

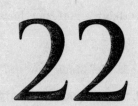

22

The buildings of Glacier City weren't anything like the quaint gingerbread houses of Rime Village or the strange, round dwellings in Dark Light. They were as drab as the muddy homes of Oak, but taller, with windows of different sizes and shapes that gave each building the appearance of its own unique, unwelcoming expression. And above them all rose the lopsided silhouette of moldering Glacier City Keep.

Evangeline pulled her cloak tightly around herself as she and Sparrow Fall wound through the dingy streets.

"Where're you off to, little sausages?" cackled a voice from the shadows of a sneering tenement.

"Oh, hobnob, I've lost my left shoe!" came a wail from atop a decrepit balcony that looked like a toothy grimace. "Whoever will help me find my left shoe?"

"Psst," Sparrow Fall whispered. "Don't try to help him find his left shoe."

"Yeah." Evangeline tugged at the hood of her cloak, making sure her face was hidden.

Sparrow Fall grinned. "The *good* news is there aren't any soldiers around here!"

Evangeline wasn't comforted by this information. "Where are we headed?"

"Near the docks," her companion said. Evangeline could hear the sea and smell the salt in the air, but the water itself was hidden somewhere beyond the crowded, menacing buildings. "Almost there."

The violet-haired fairy's eyes glimmered. Sparrow Fall seemed positively excited at the idea of staging a daring rescue in the heart of the Winter Kingdom. And it seemed to Evangeline that as they got closer to wherever it was he was leading them, the rainbows cast by Sparrow Fall's wings grew brighter, and more and more glitter cascaded off him as he darted through the air. How either of those things would be useful, she couldn't imagine.

All of a sudden, Evangeline stopped, right between a haughty pawn shop and an abandoned factory with seven squinting eyes. "Do you hear that?" she said.

The streets of Glacier City sang a discordant lament, the intertwined melodies of hoarse cries, slamming doors, the flapping of laundry and splashing of buckets being emptied, and the constant, angry wind that barreled in from the sea and got caught in the streets. But in this spot, faintly, Evangeline could hear something else—a dancing, laughing tune that cut through the noise and misery.

It was a violin. It was the violin she'd heard in Lakecrest. "Mom?" she murmured.

"What did you say?" Sparrow Fall asked.

Evangeline cocked her head, listening. "I can hear a violin playing."

"A violin?" The fairy shuddered, side to side. "No, no, no. No violins here. *No* violins." His sparkling blue face grew three shades paler.

Evangeline gave him a puzzled look. "You have a stringed instrument phobia or something?"

Sparrow Fall zoomed up to her face, buzzed close to her right ear, and whispered, "Violins are *forbidden*."

"I know, but it's just so silly! You can't really be serious," Evangeline said, more loudly than she meant to in the middle of the run-down street. A squat, scarred man with an actual beak looked up from the argument he was having with a scruffy crow perched on a stick. A woman with eyes where her nose should have been and one large ear in the middle of her forehead turned away from a window she was cleaning with a broom and stared.

Evangeline quickly started walking again. She followed the sound of the violin, which was unmistakable now. "Anyway, it may be forbidden, but I can hear it," she said to Sparrow Fall. "Can't you? The music?"

He dipped, hovering around her knees as she strode onward. "Nope, nope," he said. "I don't hear anything."

"That's not true," Evangeline scolded. She stopped outside a black, two-story building whose upper walls were riddled with tiny windows. The first floor contained no windows at all, but there was a sturdy metal door with a tarnished plaque in the middle.

Evangeline squatted down to be level with Sparrow Fall, who was still flying low. "The music's coming from in there." There could be no doubt now. Coming from behind the metal door was the sound of a violin, clear and springy.

"There is no violin music," Sparrow Fall said frantically. "Violins have been forbidden for almost twelve years!"

"I'm going to knock," Evangeline said.

"No! You can't!" Sparrow Fall zipped behind a rotten rain barrel.

Evangeline hesitated. "Then let's go. We have to find whoever this person is who can help us get into the keep."

Sparrow Fall peeked over the top with a frightened expression. "Um, actually, we're going . . . here."

Evangeline put her hands on her hips. "What? Then *someone* is not being very brave *at all* right now," she said.

The fairy glared at her. "We can't go in while—while *that* is going on! There's a difference between being brave and being an idiot!"

"Well, if the king outlawed violin music, then *he's* the idiot," Evangeline said. At this, Sparrow Fall's eyes rolled back into his head and he fell, *thump*, unconscious onto the dirty street. With a sigh, Evangeline—carefully, not knowing how rude it might be—picked him up and put him in one of the spacious pockets of her cloak. Then she knocked on the door.

A narrow strip of metal slid aside to reveal two green eyes with tall, narrow pupils like a cat's. "Password?"

Shoot, Evangeline thought. She knew nothing about what might be behind the door, or what sort of password she needed, and Sparrow Fall was out like a light.

Her eyes flicked to the tarnished plaque. It had a picture of a sandwich on it. "Uh . . . ," she said. "Sandwich?"

The cat's eyes looked at her for a moment. Then, "Okay!" *Click*, the door swung open on silky hinges.

Evangeline stepped inside. She'd thought it might be a tavern like the one in Oak, greasy and smoke-filled. But what she found was nothing like what she expected. It was a small, well-lit room with a green curtained door at the back. Sunny little tables covered with bright fabric dotted the floor, and at each one, two or three people sat. And every customer, tall or small, giraffe-horned or one-eyed or neon polka-dotted, was munching contentedly on a delicious sandwich.

"Welcome to Morris's Sandwich Shop!" the man behind the door said with a broad grin. Except for his green cat's eyes, he looked more human than anyone Evangeline had met so far in the Winter Kingdom. His dark blond hair was quite wild, and stuck out from his head like a cloud, and over his forearm was draped a blue tea towel embroidered with spoons. "Right this way!" He gestured with a large hand, and Evangeline sat down at a table. The cloth was clean and cheerful, and at the center was a small vase with a single bell-shaped orange flower. If she hadn't been distracted by what was going on at the other end of the room, Evangeline would have been delighted.

For there, standing on a low stool, her eyes closed, two of her delicate arms drawing bows across the strings of a yellow violin that shone like crystal and sang like summer, was Hortense.

23

"Hortense!" Evangeline cried before she could stop herself. But Hortense didn't seem to hear her over the chatter of customers and the sweet music of her yellow crystal violin.

Mr. Morris, the restaurant owner, smiled. "You know our little clarinetist?"

"Yes!" Evangeline couldn't believe how much her heart was jumping around in her chest. Hortense was here! Was she angry? Would she forgive her? Evangeline was excited and nervous at the same time. This must be what it felt like to have a friend. Then she turned to Mr. Morris. "Wait, but she's not playing a clarinet. It's a vi—"

"Of course it's a clarinet!" Mr. Morris boomed good-naturedly, and a few other people in the restaurant laughed. "What else could it possibly be, okay?" He leaned in, putting his big hands on Evangeline's table. "Now, what can I get you?"

"I'm looking for someone, actually," Evangeline said. "Someone special."

"Ah." Mr. Morris nodded knowingly. "Love is in the air! And what says 'I love you' more than a sandwich?"

"No, not that sort of someone special." Evangeline felt her face growing warm.

Mr. Morris leaned on his elbows. "Okay, so who do you look for, little one?"

Evangeline paused. "I . . . don't know. My friend knew, but he's asleep." She realized how stupid she must sound. She felt in her pocket and risked a little poke with her finger, but the unconscious fairy didn't stir.

"Then it's time for a sandwich!" Mr. Morris said boisterously. "Apple and gort cheese? Flapweed on honeybread? You look peaked, little one."

Evangeline realized the hood of her cloak had slipped back from her face, and she tugged it into place again. "I—" Her spirits fell. "I don't have any money." *I don't even know what money looks like here*, she thought.

Mr. Morris slapped the table and stood up. Evangeline jumped. She thought he would throw her out. But he merely grinned wider and pointed at her. "A Morris Special! Coming right up, okay?" Then he bustled back to the curtained door and disappeared into the kitchen.

Hortense finished her song and Evangeline dared to stand up and approach her while the customers applauded. Her hands shook as she crossed the clean-swept floor of the sandwich shop, but she kept going.

Hortense noticed her. Her large black eyes widened in surprise. "Evangeline?" she said, stepping down from the stool.

Evangeline pointed at the crystal violin. "So that's what you were carrying around in that bag."

Hortense's face reddened. "Yes. It's . . . it's a secret, obviously. But there are hidden places, like this, where I can still make use of it."

They were silent for a moment; something squishy and tangled hung in the air between them. Then Evangeline said, "I'm sorry for how I treated you, Hortense. It wasn't any kind of way to treat a friend. I shouldn't have left you. I shouldn't have listened to Polly."

She hoped Hortense would smile and shake hands. But instead, the arana burst into tears.

"Oh, oh!" exclaimed Mr. Morris, emerging from the kitchen with a sandwich on a plate. "Miss Hortense, the treasure of Glacier City! You need lunch, okay? Come have a sandwich." He put an arm around Hortense's shoulders and steered her across the room to Evangeline's table. He set the sandwich, which looked like peanut butter and jelly, down in front of Hortense, whose tears subsided although she still sniffled violently. "You take this one," Mr. Morris said, then pointed at Evangeline. "I'll get you another, okay?"

Evangeline smiled and nodded. As Mr. Morris strode away, she tried to think of something to say.

Hortense poked at the peanut butter and jelly. "Mr. Morris always tries to fix everything with sandwiches," she said weakly. They both laughed. "I'm sorry to cause a scene," Hortense continued, wiping her eyes, "especially when you're trying to keep a low profile. Although nobody in here would ever give you away."

"I like this place," Evangeline said as her friend took a bite of sandwich.

Hortense looked pleased. "This is where I was working when I got arrested. Luckily it wasn't a raid on the restaurant. I got caught buying violin strings from a black market street merchant." She shook her head. "Stupid!"

"I can't believe the *violin* is illegal here!" Evangeline said. "It's the most ridiculous thing I've ever heard. What reason can there possibly be?"

"I keep forgetting you're not from here," Hortense said, chewing. "The king decreed the violin to be forbidden twelve years ago, when the queen died. She had played the violin, you see, and it broke his heart to hear the instrument."

"The queen," Evangeline murmured. "My mother."

Hortense nodded. "I'm sorry to bring it up."

"My mother's still alive," Evangeline said, which made Hortense raise her eyebrows in surprise. "Why did she go to Earth? And why did she leave Desdemona here with our father, when he's such a monster?"

"I don't know," Hortense said, and suddenly seemed far away. She put a hand on her crystal violin, which was sitting next to her on the table.

"Another Morris Special, okay!" With a flourish, the restaurant owner set a plate down in front of Evangeline, as well as two tall glasses of a sparkling green liquid garnished with blue cherries.

"Thank you, Mr. Morris," Evangeline said.

"Huh?" came a muffled voice from within the folds of her cloak.

Mr. Morris raised an eyebrow theatrically. "The stowaway stirs!"

Two curly golden horns and a billow of violet hair poked over the top of Evangeline's pocket. "Where—?" Sparrow Fall said groggily.

"A fairy!" Mr. Morris exclaimed. "And if it isn't my good friend, the sparrow who falls." He plucked the skewer of blue cherries out of Evangeline's drink and laid it down on a napkin. "Now he can eat, too, okay?" And the big, wild-haired man scooted away.

Hortense grew quite pale. She got to her feet. "I should go, before—"

A miniature scream erupted from Evangeline's pocket. *"Arana!"*

"Yes," Hortense said. "That."

A few customers looked over to see what was the matter. Evangeline hissed into her cloak, "Hey, this is my friend Hortense! Just because you're not brave doesn't mean you have to be rude. Show some manners."

"I'm sorry," Sparrow Fall said meekly, finally emerging. "You're right." He took a graceful fly-leap onto the table and walked over to where Hortense was standing, looking at his feet the whole time. He extended a trembling blue hand. "I'm p . . . pleased to meet you."

Hortense seated herself and held out two eggshell-nailed fingers. They shook hands.

Then Sparrow Fall looked up. He blinked, tilted his head, and blinked again. "You *are* an arana, aren't you?" he asked.

Hortense nodded, with a puzzled look on her face. "The eight limbs are a clue," she said.

"Yes," Sparrow Fall said. He seemed to be thinking. "People in my village told stories about aranae coming in the night and stealing fairies to make into soup."

"Well," Hortense said, as the scene was getting more awkward. "That's great." She focused on her sandwich.

Evangeline wished the fairy would get over whatever was on his mind so he could find the mysterious person who could help them. She was about to say so when Sparrow Fall spoke again. "But—I don't understand. You're not at all like they said." He peered at Hortense. "You're *beautiful*."

Hortense didn't seem to know how to respond to this. She just stared at Sparrow Fall with her eyebrows furrowed.

Evangeline swallowed a mouthful of sandwich. It did taste a lot like peanut butter and jelly, only the peanut butter was a little more flowery and the jelly tingled as though it were carbonated. "Sir Paw-on-Stone has been captured by the Lord High Keeper," she said, "but Sparrow Fall knows someone who can get us into Glacier City Keep."

Sparrow Fall seemed to break out of his trance and settled, cross-legged, by the napkin of blue cherries.

"Then we'd better hurry up and finish our sandwiches," Hortense said.

"Wait—*we*?" Evangeline said, leaning forward.

Hortense shrugged and smiled, a blob of jelly stuck to one of her long fangs. "Of course!"

Mr. Morris scooted up to their table again, pulling up a chair this time. "Now that we have happy sandwich bellies, what can I do to help you, my friends? Who is this special person you look for, okay?"

Sparrow Fall tilted his head, blue cherry juice running over his chin. "Special person?" He looked from Evangeline to Hortense to Mr. Morris. "It's you, of course, Mr. Morris. We need help getting into the—" He lowered his voice. "The *dungeon of Glacier City Keep*."

The cat-eyed man with the wild hair rocked back in his little café chair and laughed. "You always make me laugh, tiny horned rainbow friend!"

"We're serious," Evangeline said. "Please."

Mr. Morris studied her solemn face. "I see that you are, little one. But why can a princess not simply walk through the front door?"

Evangeline blinked. "You know who I am?"

Mr. Morris frowned. "Yes and no, little one. Yes and no."

24

Night fell quickly over Glacier City, filling the streets with crooked, inky shadows. Evangeline, Hortense, and Sparrow Fall followed Mr. Morris out the back door of his secret sandwich shop to a quiet edge of the city docks.

"Here," Mr. Morris said, stopping behind a bunch of barrels covered by a thick net. He put his big hands on his hips. "Now, you tell me what this is about, okay?"

Evangeline looked up at his shining cat eyes. He looked harmless, friendly. But so had Polly. Sparrow Fall trusted Mr. Morris, but who was Sparrow Fall, really? Her insides swirled.

Then she felt thin, hairy fingers grasping hers. Hortense gave her a shining-fang smile, then turned to Mr. Morris. "Evangeline is new to the Winter Kingdom. She needs to travel beyond the Crystal Gate, but it's locked and the last Keeper—the only one who can unlock it—is trapped in the dungeon of Glacier City Keep. We have to rescue him."

Mr. Morris's cat pupils grew black with concern. "The last Keeper? What do you mean, last? What has happened to them?"

"They've been accidentally getting themselves killed," Evangeline said. "My sister, Princess Desdemona, thought there was something shady going on. Now it's clear King Vair has been behind it all."

Mr. Morris looked up at the pinprick stars that poked through the Glacier City mist. He spoke as if to himself. "So, in truth, two Keepers remain: the white fox is loyal to the princess; the ice troll is loyal to the king." He turned to Evangeline. "Your friend is in danger."

"We know," Sparrow Fall said with a puff of glitter. "And we're out of time. Can you help us?"

Mr. Morris sank his wide chin into his chest, frowning and thinking. "The keep has many safeguards against thieves and jailbreaks," he murmured. Then he looked up. "Portal. It's the only way."

"A portal?" Sparrow Fall was aghast. "I thought you'd suggest, I don't know, dressing up like guards or hiding in the laundry baskets or something."

"You want to hide in the laundry, go ahead." Mr. Morris shrugged. "But you will be discovered. They jab with sharp sticks!" He made a jabbing motion. "Glacier City Keep is one of the most carefully guarded places in the whole Winter Kingdom. If we had a week, I could think of something else."

"We don't have a week," Evangeline said. "Sir Paw-on-Stone might have sealed the Crystal Gate from portals, but King Vair can open it with the rootball stone and he's on his way right now!" She couldn't keep the shake from her voice.

"The rootball stone?" Mr. Morris's green eyes grew panicked. "Oh dear! That is not good. Not good at all!"

"He has it, I know he does," Evangeline said. "I felt them find it. Now he sees my sister and me as threats to his immortal rule."

"Are you?" Sparrow Fall asked. "Because, honestly, a threat to his immortal rule would be nice right about now."

The fairy's earnest face stopped Evangeline's words for a moment. But she regained herself. "I'm just a girl who came here to save her sister. I don't know anything about fixing the problems of a whole kingdom. I just want to get Desdemona out of here and back to Earth, where no crazed kings will turn us into ice sculptures!"

Mr. Morris nodded. "Then portal."

"It's too risky!" Sparrow Fall zipped from barrel to barrel, fretting.

"We have no choice," Hortense said with fire in her black-orb eyes. "Princess Desdemona only has just over a day left before the king reaches the Crystal Gate."

Evangeline ran her hand along a net-draped crate. She traced the rope knots, tiny jets of ice sparking from her fingers and burrowing in between the fibers. If Glacier City Keep was as impenetrable as Mr. Morris thought it was, a portal was the only way. She turned to the cat-eyed man. "All right. Mr. Morris, we need you to open your portal now."

The cat eyes widened. "Me?" He laughed. "Do I look like I can work portal magic?" He put a big hand on Evangeline's shoulder. "No, no, no. Only sandwich magic."

Evangeline's heart sank. "But—"

"*You* must open the portal, little one," Mr. Morris said. "You are a princess of the Winter Kingdom, okay? Its power is yours, not mine."

"Me?" Evangeline threw up her hands. The frozen netting over the barrels behind her shattered. "I don't know how to open a portal!"

Mr. Morris smiled. "How came you from Terra? You did not ride a cow-bear."

"I—" Evangeline paused. "It was a little confusing. But I'm sure it was my sister who did something to the mirror in my room, not me." *It was, wasn't it?* she thought. *There's no way I created that mirror portal . . . is there?*

"Well, we try," Mr. Morris said, shrugging. "How do we know if we do not try, okay?"

"Mr. Morris is very wise," Sparrow Fall chimed in. "I knew he could help us."

"You can do it, Evangeline," Hortense said. The creak of ships in harbor rose above the misty quiet. Orange lamplight flickered over the worn barrels, the rough wooden planking, the heaps of rotting mulch and damp shreds of rope that littered the Glacier City docks.

"I will help, okay?" Mr. Morris said. "To travel with the mirrors between worlds, that is hard. No Keeper, and not even King Vair, can do that. But for a princess to travel in her own land—that is easy."

Evangeline wasn't so sure. Mr. Morris stood behind her and put a heavy hand on each of her shoulders. "Look straight ahead. Do not look *at*, look *through*."

Evangeline stared at the pile of sea-worn barrels, trying not to focus on them. It felt a bit like daydreaming in class.

"This is your kingdom," Mr. Morris said, his voice slow and even. "Just as you are a part of it, *it* is a part of *you*."

Evangeline kept breathing the briny air. In. Out. In. Out. She closed her eyes. Or did she?

"Feel the land, the air, the cold clouds."

Evangeline's skin tingled in the damp sea air. She felt the wooden planks beneath her feet, then the individual granules of salt that clung there. And then . . . she could feel the planks touching the barnacle-encrusted pilings that stretched down into the dark, rippling water of the harbor. She felt the vegetable-strewn streets of Glacier City and the dry, sand-lodged rocks beyond. She kept feeling, sensing, sending tendrils of herself farther and farther away—snowy forests, proud ridges of mountains, clear lakes sparkling like diamonds, small villages with deep wells, towns that vibrated with urgency, Bright Mine itself, which—which—which *yearned* for something through a haze of fear, and finally the place that looked like a blanket of green-gray mushrooms in a drift of snow, the town that hugged the white palace on the hill.

"Find the keep," Mr. Morris said.

In her mind, Evangeline traveled the edges of Glacier City. She floated up the frost-webbed wall of the black keep that rose in the middle, then dove, down, down, around twisting torchlit stairwells and through musty underground passageways, until at last she came to a dark, sad place where even the air had been forgotten.

"I found the dungeon," she whispered.

"Excellent," Mr. Morris said. "Now, the land is a great, frosty blanket. You are here, at this edge. The dungeon of Glacier City Keep is there, at that edge. Grasp the edge, little one, and fold. Pull the dungeon to you."

Evangeline breathed out. She reached out a hand. It was her real hand, but also the spectral hand in her mind. Her fingers pulled at the sea breeze of Glacier City, at the vast, shining blanket that was the skin of the Winter Kingdom. Her fingers were bones and clouds and dense snow.

"Okay!" Mr. Morris clapped. Evangeline opened her eyes. Before her, the air shimmered. But unlike the Lord High Keeper's greasy portal, or Sir Paw-on-Stone's shivering one, Evangeline's portal was bright and sharp. It looked like a hundred mirrors talking about light with one another, crisscrossing beams of vibrant colors and hints of scenes from every place imaginable. And beyond, a gloomy pit of square stones and rot.

Sparrow Fall zoomed around in blurry rainbow figure eights. "You did it!"

"Wow!" Hortense said, peering into the portal. "It doesn't look like anyone's around. We should take our chance now."

"Agreed," said Sparrow Fall in a shaky voice.

Hortense turned to Mr. Morris and held out the long bag that contained her yellow crystal violin. "Will you keep it safe for me?" He nodded. Then Hortense straightened her spine, took a deep breath, and strode through the portal, vaporizing into the air as she passed the shimmering borders.

"Wait—!" Evangeline started. "Mr. Morris, she's gone! Is she okay?"

"Of course!" Mr. Morris said. "It is a thing of beauty, this portal. Well done, Your Highness. Too bad it won't last. But you have no time to lose, in any case."

Evangeline shook his big hand. "Thank you."

He waved her away. "Get to the keep, little one. I will serve you all my finest sandwiches when next we meet!"

Sparrow Fall buzzed the edges of the portal tentatively. "I'll follow, if it's all the same to you."

Evangeline gave a last wave to Mr. Morris and stepped through the portal.

There was no stomach-lurching topsy-turviness this time, not even a rush of wind. It was like stepping into a pool. In no time at all, Evangeline slid out the other side of the portal into the dark, dingy dungeon of the old keep.

As her feet touched down on the stone floor, Sparrow Fall zoomed in after her and sped away down the dim passageway. Evangeline checked her portal; it was still shimmering in the air. But it wouldn't last forever.

"I don't see any guards," Hortense whispered in the gloom. "There's not much reason for them to be down here, I guess. There's no way in or out, except through the keep itself."

"Lucky for us," Evangeline whispered.

Sparrow Fall came streaking back down the low stone hallway. "I found your friend," he said, out of breath. "I can't get him out alone. He's in a cage. He's . . . not very talkative."

The fairy led the way, with Evangeline and Hortense running after him. Around the first corner, they came to an open prison cell with thick bars and slime dripping from the walls. In one dark corner sat a cage no bigger than a school desk, its door fastened with a heavy padlock, smooth and brown. Sparrow Fall hovered next to it, casting an eerie light over the scene and jerking forward and back, as though he were pacing. Inside the cage was Sir Paw-on-Stone.

"Oh!" Evangeline croaked at the sight of him. She rushed across the stones and knelt next to the cage. The white fox within was sitting on his haunches, and he looked over at her with large golden eyes. But he didn't seem to recognize her. In fact, he didn't seem to be thinking much at all about anything that was going on. Evangeline wondered if he were even really looking *at* her, or just gazing mindlessly in her direction. His stately purple cape was rumpled and hanging crookedly, half over his shoulders, half bunched under his paws. Around his neck was fastened a heavy collar of emeralds set in bronze. He didn't say a word.

25

"Sir Paw-on-Stone?" Evangeline asked, her voice echoing in the cold dungeon. But the white fox in the cage didn't move, or even blink. She called on her powers, throwing the coldest ice she could muster at the little metal door, but unlike the cage on the road, these bars would not break. It was as though they were protected by some kind of magic.

Sparrow Fall flitted this way and that, and Sir Paw-on-Stone seemed vaguely interested for a moment, the way a dog might raise his head if someone waved a mediocre treat from rather far away. Then, with a vacant expression, Sir Paw-on-Stone, last surviving Keeper of the Crystal Gate, stuck his hindquarters into the air, stretched a massive stretch, and settled down to sleep, his head resting on his front paws.

"Hey!" Evangeline rattled the bars. One golden eye opened. "It's me, Evangeline! You locked the Crystal Gate to protect Princess Desdemona, and you promised to unlock it and get me through to her. We're here to get you out!"

The other eye opened, and they both peered at Evangeline with a little more shrewdness. But the fox still said nothing.

"It's the mortal band," Hortense whispered.

"I did wonder what would happen if one were forced onto a Keeper," said Sparrow Fall.

"Why?" Evangeline said. She rose, scanning the walls for hanging keys.

The fairy buzzed along next to her, his wings stirring the dust that had gathered in the corners and crevices of the dungeon. "You see, mortal bands dampen magic, as I said. Most folks have a little magic in them. The bands take the edge off, make people easier to catch and control. But Keepers—they're *mostly* magic."

Evangeline paused, casting a glance at the fox in the cage. "So, that means he's mostly gone," she whispered.

"I don't think he'll come with us willingly," Hortense said. "I don't think he cares."

"We've got to him out of there." Evangeline found a long piece of sturdy metal—some kind of torture device, or maybe just part of a desk or something—and jammed it between the little barred door and the top of the cage. "Unff!" she groaned, pressing all her weight onto the makeshift lever. Hortense helped, and they pushed and pulled until the long piece of metal bent. The cage door was as solid as ever. Sir Paw-on-Stone closed his eyes.

Suddenly, a *clank* echoed through the lonely subterranean hall. Everyone froze, listening. Sparrow Fall alighted on Evangeline's shoulder and cocked his ear.

"Someone's coming!" Evangeline whispered. "We've got to go *now*."

"How do we get him out? We have no key!" Sparrow Fall zoomed around the room, running his hands between the moldy stones where secret things might be hidden.

"All right," Evangeline said. "We have no key."

"What are our options?" asked Hortense.

"Panic?" said Sparrow Fall shakily. "Weep? Screech?"

But Evangeline was done panicking, fretting, overthinking. *Key*, she thought. She touched the smooth padlock. She'd seen criminals and plucky amateur detectives pick locks like this on TV. They'd unroll a leather sleeve of slim, fancy tools, or sometimes just pluck a bobby pin from their hair. Evangeline didn't have slim tools or hair accessories. And she didn't have much time, either.

What do *I have?* she thought. Her fingers twitched. She breathed in the dank air. *I have ice.*

She held the padlock and ran her thumb over the keyhole. *Key*, she thought. *Key.* And the ice came. It crackled from under her fingernails and seeped into the keyhole, filling the space, crystallizing into the perfect shape. She couldn't help a smile of satisfaction. Her ice-key even had a fancy little handle. She turned it.

Click. The ice-key worked flawlessly. The padlock fell open.

Suddenly, the sound of a door creaking cut through the dungeon. Evangeline, Hortense, and Sparrow Fall looked at one another, then silently dove for whatever cover they could find. The fairy squeezed behind a lit torch, his light blending with the flame. Evangeline ducked beneath the remains of a decrepit wooden platform chained to the wall of the prison cell opposite Sir Paw-on-Stone's. And Hortense scuttled up the wall itself, clinging to a black corner of the ceiling.

A moment later, footsteps approached, a slow *thump* . . . *thump* . . . *thump* echoing down the quiet hallway.

"How is our guest?" rumbled the last voice Evangeline wanted to hear right now.

"Quiet as a snowman, Lord High Keeper," a scratchy voice answered. "He's got nothing to say now."

The footsteps drew nearer. Evangeline tensed her body, certain the Lord High Keeper would be able to hear her heart thumping against the floorboards. He stalked into view, his wide shadow interrupting the meager light from the one lit torch that spilled into Evangeline's hiding place. She hoped with all her bones he wouldn't notice that the padlock on the fox's cage was not quite as closed as it ought to have been.

"Enjoying your stay, Fourth Keeper?" the Lord High Keeper boomed. Evangeline couldn't see Sir Paw-on-Stone, but there was no reply from the fox to the ice troll.

"What should we do with him?" asked the raspy voice. A tendril of pipe smoke crawled under the wooden platform, stinging Evangeline's nostrils. She held her breath so she wouldn't sneeze.

"Just—" the Lord High Keeper began, then stopped. There was a long pause. Evangeline watched the hem of his long black coat swish this way and that, as though he were looking around, listening. Then he asked, in a quiet, dangerous voice, "Are you *certain* no one unknown to you has entered the keep during the last day, Captain?"

Evangeline closed her eyes. She didn't want him to hear her blink.

The raspy voice coughed. "Absolutely certain, Lord High Keeper!"

"No new delivery girls? No charities knocking on the door? No fire safety inspections?"

"None at all," said the captain. "I'd stake my life on it!"

"Would you?" the Lord High Keeper rumbled. "Would you, indeed? Well, that's excellent, sir."

Another puff of pipe smoke wound its way underneath the wooden platform and into Evangeline's nose. She felt the tingle of a sneeze, fiercer and fiercer. She clamped down her lungs and pressed her lips together.

After another moment, the echoing footsteps made their way back down the long hall, away from Sir Paw-on-Stone's cell and the adjacent hallway where Evangeline hoped her portal would still be waiting for them.

"That was too close," Evangeline muttered, rolling out from under the platform. Sparrow Fall sidled out from behind the torch and Hortense dropped silently from the ceiling.

Evangeline rushed to Sir Paw-on-Stone's unlocked cage and yanked the door open. "Let's go." The fox opened his eyes and looked up at her, but didn't move. "We've got to get the mortal band off him," Evangeline said.

"I can do it," Hortense said, reaching for the ornate ring of emeralds and brass. But to everyone's surprise, he growled, showing his dangerous fangs. His ears flattened against his head and his eyes grew black. Hortense pulled her hand back. "Hey! I'm trying to help you!"

Sparrow Fall zipped over. "Allow me." He flitted inside the cage, hovering a few inches from the white fox's face. Sir Paw-on-Stone growled again, louder. Evangeline gasped. The fox could easily snap the little fairy up with one bite.

"Peace, my friend," Sparrow Fall said, and his wide wings relaxed from a flutter to a slow, mesmerizing pulse. Then he reached out a small hand and placed it on the tip of the white fox's nose.

The fox's pupils shrank back to their normal size, his golden irises glimmering. His ears unclenched, popping back up into their naturally friendly position. And his mouth closed, hiding sharp fangs behind soft white whiskers.

"There we are," Sparrow Fall said. "There is nothing to fear." Without lifting his one hand from Sir Paw-on-Stone's nose, he beckoned Hortense with the other.

Carefully, she reached two of her hands toward the fox's head, *closer, closer,* until she reached the clasp of the heavy emerald necklace. Then, with a quick click and prod, the mortal band snapped open and fell onto the metal floor of the cage with a *clunk.*

"You did it!" Evangeline cried as Sparrow Fall flitted out of the cage.

"That was amazing!" Hortense said. "What did you do?"

It seemed to Evangeline that the fairy actually blushed a little, a hint of purple spreading over his blue cheeks. "It's not much of a talent," he said. "I mean, it's not conjuring blizzards or anything. But I've always been good at—I don't know. Peacefulness."

"I think it's a great talent," Evangeline said, glancing at Sir Paw-on-Stone. Then she frowned. "What's the matter with him, though?" The fox was unruffled, but there was still no sign that he recognized them.

Sparrow Fall bobbed in the air, droopy. "It . . . might be too late. He might be gone."

"No," Hortense murmured.

Evangeline put a hand to the fox's fluffy jowl. "Please." The golden eyes looked into hers as though she were a stranger.

"Having problems with your friend?" a voice like a mountain thundered in the dark dungeon.

At the far end of the hallway loomed an enormous shape. In the gloom, patches of dirty light glinted off hard ice-white skin.

Evangeline jumped and let out a cry. Hortense's crystal-ball eyes widened. Sparrow Fall zipped upward so dramatically he smashed into the ceiling and fell to the floor, the wind knocked out of him.

"At last I find the fugitive princess, conveniently hiding in my own dungeon," the Lord High Keeper bellowed. "You will not escape me again."

For a split second, Evangeline braced herself for a jet of magical ice to come streaking down the grimy hallway. Her arms flew to her face, muscles tensed; she gritted her teeth. But to her surprise, the Lord High Keeper did something far more terrifying.

He began to *charge*.

He raced toward them down the stone passageway, which was barely large enough for him to fit through. The ice troll didn't lope or lumber, he flew like a freight train. His velvet hat brushed the ceiling and his shoulders knocked into the walls on both sides, scraping granules from the mortar between the stones that clattered onto the floor.

Evangeline forced herself to snap out of her stupor. She dropped her arms and kicked her body into action. "Run!" she yelled, snatching Sir Paw-on-Stone while Hortense scooped up Sparrow Fall. They both dashed down the murky hall, slipping on muck, toward where they hoped the portal was still open. Behind them echoed the thunderous footfalls of the fearsome Lord High Keeper.

Evangeline was relieved to catch sight of the portal's shimmer as she skidded around the corner—but it was fading fast. Perhaps only a few more seconds. "Go!" she yelled.

Hortense leapt ahead on nimble legs and dove through headfirst. She was through!

Evangeline clung tight to the white fox as she barreled toward the rapidly fading portal—*five more steps . . . three . . .*

"Arrrrrgh!" the Lord High Keeper roared, lunging. He managed to grab ahold of Evangeline's long cloak and gave it a ferocious pull. Evangeline staggered backward, tossing Sir Paw-on-Stone through the portal.

I can't fail now! she thought. The portal was little more than a slight glimmer in the shadows of the dungeon. The Lord High Keeper had a firm hold on her cloak as she tried frantically to wriggle out of it.

"You'll look nice in the king's sculpture garden, Your Highness," the ice troll sneered. He grasped the edge of Evangeline's cloak with one massive hand and yanked, grabbing the fabric farther up with the other hand. Evangeline scrabbled against the slick floor of the dungeon as the Lord High Keeper yanked again, pulling her back from the fading portal as though he were climbing her cloak like a rope.

Then Evangeline had a scrap of an idea. Closing her eyes, she called on *ice*, squeezing it out of her pores, through her clothes, and into the fibers of the long cloak.

In a flash, the cloak froze solid, then shattered in the Lord High Keeper's hands. As Evangeline leapt through the last remnants of the portal, she heard him bellow in rage.

26

Sir Paw-on-Stone was still silent and glassy-eyed. He alternated between staring vacantly at the colorful sandwich menu on the wall of Mr. Morris's restaurant and sleeping curled up in a bread basket. The restaurant was closed for the night, but Mr. Morris had set them up with blankets on the floor. There had been no sign of the Lord High Keeper. He hadn't gotten through the portal and had no idea where it had led.

Evangeline watched Sir Paw-on-Stone, twisting her fingers. "There *has* to be some way to bring him back," she said. "To bring his magic back." *So we can get to Princess Desdemona*, she thought, then looked out the window at the moon. *By tomorrow.*

Sparrow Fall shrugged. "He has his magic. He had it as soon as we got the mortal band off."

"So why is he still—you know," Evangeline said. "Like that." Sir Paw-on-Stone got to his feet and casually lifted his leg all over the bread basket and his lovely purple cape.

"What was it like when you had the band on?" Hortense asked. Sparrow Fall drifted in a circle.

"Well, I wasn't exactly using my powers yet," Evangeline said. "But it was very heavy. I'm not sure where his mind is. Maybe we can snap him out of it? Maybe we can, I don't know, jolt him back here?"

"How?" Hortense asked.

Evangeline sat back, resting against a table leg carved to look like a tentacle. "What about something familiar?"

Sparrow Fall's circular flight became more animated. "It's worth a shot, right?"

"But what?" Evangeline wished she knew more about Sir Paw-on-Stone. What were his favorite things, his hobbies? What memories were important to him?

Then she had an idea. "Let's try this!" she said, pulling out a small object from the pocket of her corduroys. "Look," she said, holding the object out to the white fox in the basket. It did seem to catch his attention. He sniffed it cautiously. "Remember this?" Evangeline asked.

The fox kept sniffing, eyeing, twitching his fluffy tail. Suddenly, he barked.

"Bruff!"

Evangeline grinned. "Yes! Yes, what is it?"

"Bruff!" the fox barked again. His eyes jumped from the object to

Evangeline's face and back again. "Juff! JUFF!" Now he was half bark-ing, half growling, getting agitated.

"Maybe we should try later," Hortense said.

"No," Evangeline said over her shoulder. "He almost has it!"

"J—JELLY BEAN HUGS!" Sir Paw-on-Stone blurted out.

Everyone cheered. The white fox sat on his haunches with a pleased expression. After a moment, he wrinkled his nose. "What smells like pee?"

❄ ❄ ❄

Sir Paw-on-Stone was himself, mostly, but very weak, so they decided to sleep for a couple of hours on the floor of the restaurant, just until dawn. Evangeline tucked the fox into a basket. "You do *not* have the proper clearance to lay a hand upon a . . . a . . . ," he slurred, then wrapped his fuzzy tail over his face and began to snore.

Hortense crawled under a table and curled into a ball, tucking her arms and legs underneath her. Sparrow Fall asked if anyone was inter-ested in snuggling, casting a hopeful glance in the arana's direction, but nobody answered him. He disappeared with a shrug, but after a few minutes, Evangeline heard what might have been tiny, whistling snores coming from the chandelier above them.

Finally, Evangeline gathered a colorful afghan and snugged her-self into a corner. She was so tired, she thought she'd fall asleep immediately. But her mind wouldn't turn off. What would she do if Sir Paw-on-Stone was still too weak to help her in the morning? And even if she reached Princess Desdemona—and this new thought made her shoulders slump and her lungs ache—how could she be sure they even *could* create a portal back to Earth?

Then she thought of Hortense and Sparrow Fall and Sir Paw-on-Stone, who couldn't possibly fit in back home. They would be left behind. They had all defied King Vair by helping Evangeline. It would be her fault if he brought his wrath down upon them. She remembered the terrifying, frigid, spike-toothed smile of the Lord High Keeper, and the wretched, dripping ice sculptures in the palace garden.

Evangeline had wanted nothing more than to get out of Crestlake and Greenfield and Deer Valley and all the other boring, identical towns her mother had dragged her to. She remembered wanting to *shine*, wanting to *be* somebody.

Well, she thought, *you're somebody here. And it's hard.* Maybe that was what her mother had meant when she said people who want to be the center of attention eventually pay for it. Maybe that was why her mother had abandoned the Winter Kingdom and the ice-blue gown and the Tree of Ancient Amethyst.

Maybe Evangeline was doing exactly what her mother had been trying to protect her from her entire life.

27

"It's not like conjuring up a hole in the wall, you know," Sir Paw-on-Stone said snootily. Evangeline was glad he was back to his old self, but he did have a bit of an attitude. After far too little sleep, the four of them had gathered in a secluded curve in the shoreline near Glacier City that Mr. Morris knew about.

The white fox was painstakingly drawing circles and dots and angles and all kinds of other shapes and squiggles in the wet sand with his paws. "We're going through the Crystal Gate itself, which protects the most magical and sacred parts of the Winter Kingdom," he said. "And I must break the lock I placed on it first, before the portal will work. This isn't how I usually do it, especially not with three other people."

"Do you think King Vair is there yet?" Hortense asked.

"I don't . . . think so," the fox said, swishing a claw across the sand. "Soon."

Evangeline drew her own meaningless shape in the sand with a toe. "Will the rootball stone really open the gate?"

Sir Paw-on-Stone paused his meticulous sketching long enough to roll his eyes at her. *He's definitely back to normal,* she thought.

"The rootball stone is the source of life and energy for the whole of the world, Winter and Summer Kingdoms alike," he said, adding sarcastically, "I think it can open the gate surrounding its own tree."

"Let's hope your special portal gets us in and out before that happens," Sparrow Fall chimed nervously.

"A special portal. Like a mirror portal?" asked Evangeline, secretly proud that she knew something about the magical workings of the Winter Kingdom.

"A mirror portal?" said Hortense. "Only very powerful creatures can work mirror portals. And they're mostly used for traveling between entire *worlds*."

Very powerful creatures, Evangeline thought. *Am I a very powerful creature?*

"Anyway, the Crystal Gate only responds to portals created by its Keepers," Hortense said. "So a mirror portal wouldn't work."

"You certainly know a lot about it," Sir Paw-on-Stone said, casting a dubious glance.

Hortense stood up very straight. "Yes, I do," she said, and

Evangeline was shocked by the fire in her tone. But she didn't say any more, and neither did Sir Paw-on-Stone.

Sparrow Fall alighted on Evangeline's shoulder. "Once there were thirteen Keepers of the Crystal Gate," he murmured. "One from each of the twelve provinces of the Winter Kingdom, and one from the aranae. When King Vair took control of Bright Mine and kicked the aranae out, he—well, he had their Keeper executed."

Something clicked in Evangeline's brain. "I remember—Hortense told me that. And Taranta Lily talked about paying the king back for what he'd done to the aranae."

"Yes." Hortense sat down on a driftwood log. "Many aranae used to live near Bright Mine. It was called Bright Village then. But the king evicted us and sent us to Gnashing in the swamp, where there was hardly room and work even for the people who already lived there. I suppose that was when his miners started digging toward the rootball stone. The aranae would never have stood for it."

Evangeline sat next to her. "I had no idea. Do you remember it?"

"I was very small," Hortense said as Sparrow Fall landed on her other side. "It was around the time the queen died—sorry, when she left, when violins became outlawed. So it was a double blow for us, because my parents weren't miners. They were violin makers."

"Your crystal violin," Evangeline whispered.

"Yes." Hortense bunched the fabric of her dress in her fingers. "They didn't know anything else. They had no choice but to keep making violins, even though it was forbidden. They kept making their crystal instruments and hoping." Hortense was quiet for a long moment. Evangeline and Sparrow Fall were quiet with her. Then she said, "My yellow violin is all I have left of them."

"It's ready," came an officious little voice. Evangeline looked up to find Sir Paw-on-Stone standing proudly in the midst of his elaborate design on the sand. "We'd better hurry," he said. "The magic fades quickly." Then he looked a bit embarrassed. "And the, uh, tide's coming in and smudging my runes. I may have forgotten to factor that in."

"What should we do?" Evangeline asked.

"Come here," the white fox said, and everyone stepped gingerly across the delicate sand drawings. "Now, just hang on to me." Evangeline and Hortense knelt and placed hands on his soft fur. Sparrow Fall settled on the back of the fox's neck, one leg on each side, as though he were about to ride him in a race. Sir Paw-on-Stone made a *harrumph* kind of noise, but didn't complain. "All right," he said. "Let's go find the Tree of Ancient Amethyst."

He closed his eyes, and Evangeline's fingers were warmed by his fur. Then, as he had done at Bright Mine, he began to glow. His fur became warmer and warmer, until it was so hot, Evangeline wasn't sure she could hold on to it any longer. The white fox glowed brighter, and seemed to splinter at the edges. His face was a blur, his form jerking this way and that, but if Evangeline closed her eyes, she could feel that he wasn't actually moving. Then there was a sound like a tremendous rush of water, and Sir Paw-on-Stone's glow exploded into fiery sparks that zapped Evangeline's skin and singed her hair. All went black, then purple, then gold, then white. And at the end of it, Evangeline felt something pressing against her, as though she were splayed on the surface of a giant bubble, which popped, sending her rolling backward onto the snow.

Snow!

Had they done it? Were they through the Crystal Gate? Was Desdemona *here*? Evangeline grinned. The thought of finally meeting her sister was better than all the birthday parties and waffle dinners and chorus solos in the world.

She sat up. They were no longer at the beach near Glacier City. All around were jagged blue and purple rocks, like giant eagles' talons poking out of the snow. The air was different here. Evangeline breathed in until her lungs threatened to burst. The *air*! There was no trace of salt left, or of city. Not even pine. There was no trace of anything in this air except *ice* and *snow* and *space*—a vast space, like the sky itself. They were beyond the Crystal Gate at last, at the very summit of Bright Mountain. Evangeline jumped to her feet and ran into the strong wind, her clothes billowing and her hair streaming out behind her. She threw her head back and took another huge, gulping breath. *This* was the true Winter Kingdom!

"Whoa!" A hand grasped her shoulder. Startled, she turned to find Hortense, who pointed.

Evangeline's right foot was six inches from the edge of a very tall cliff. She looked down. There was nothing below but a few more jutting rocks and . . . clouds. Just clouds.

"Oh," Evangeline said. "Thanks."

Hortense nodded, looking a bit shocked.

"Um—could use a hand!" A voice rose above the rush of air. Sparrow Fall was floating, tumbling in place as he struggled against the wind. Hortense snatched the fairy from the air and put him in her pocket. "Thank you," he said, draping his arms out over the edge.

"This way!" Sir Paw-on-Stone called. He stood far from the edge of the mountain, beckoning them with a dainty paw. Then he disappeared between two blue rocks.

Evangeline and Hortense ran after him. When they reached the other side of the rocks, Evangeline stopped and stared. "Oh no!" she cried.

For there, before them, stood a purple tree. Only it wasn't the glorious, shining tree Evangeline remembered from her mother's photograph, or from her visions of Desdemona. It was stunted and dark, almost black, and its bark seemed to flow in bulbous glops. It had no leaves and no sparkle. It looked very, very old. And quite dead.

"Is this—this *can't* be the Tree of Ancient Amethyst?" Evangeline said.

"Well, what *else* would it be?" snapped Sir Paw-on-Stone in a voice whose edges were frayed with fear. He peered uncertainly at the dark tree. "It just looks . . . different."

"But it's supposed to shine!" Evangeline said. "It shines and spreads at the top like a canopy, and there's a cracked boulder on either side, and a waterfall behind! I saw it!"

"It's dying," Sparrow Fall murmured like a mourning dove. "The king shouldn't have taken its rootball stone."

"We're too late," Hortense said, then looked away.

"Where is Desdemona?" Evangeline cried. *"Where is my sister?"*

Sir Paw-on-Stone lay down on the snow. "I don't know," he said bitterly. "By the time I realized . . . when I found out the last two Keepers had been killed . . ." He shook his head. "I should have acted earlier. I should have listened to the *real* princess."

The real princess. The words struck Evangeline's stomach like a crossbow bolt. A real princess would be a leader, would be smart, have a plan like Desdemona. A real princess would know what to do now.

"I'm sorry," Evangeline murmured. Then a hint of anger rose in her throat. "But you could have helped me right away," she said to the fox. "You could have believed me right from the beginning."

"How was I to know you were telling the truth?" Sir Paw-on-Stone barked. "I needed *time*—"

"We didn't have time!" Evangeline said, pounding her fist against a jagged blue rock. "You could have told me more. You could have left us a better message at the tavern."

Now Sir Paw-on-Stone stopped, a puzzled expression on his face. "At the tavern? In Oak?"

Hortense looked over, curious.

"Yes," Evangeline said. "You left us that nonsense message instead of speaking plainly."

"I *always* speak plainly," the white fox said, sitting back on his haunches. "If you're too thick to understand 'Wait for me here,' then I don't know—"

"What?" Evangeline interrupted.

Hortense took a few steps toward them. "That's not the message we got," she said.

Sir Paw-on-Stone blinked. "Well, if you listened to that awful little barmaid—"

"No," Evangeline said. "I mean, yes, Polly gave us a fake message in order to trick us. But the bartender gave us your real message." She looked at the fox's perplexed face. "Except I guess it wasn't your real message."

"Why would he do that?" Sir Paw-on-Stone scratched behind his ear, thoughtful. "He seemed like a perfectly decent fellow. The drinks were a bit terrible, of course." He looked up. "What *did* he tell you?"

"'Follow your heart,'" Evangeline said.

"Follow your—does that sound like something I'd say?" Sir Paw-on-Stone asked.

"Not really." Evangeline studied the gloopy outline of the Tree of Ancient Amethyst. "But what could it mean? And why did the bartender say it?" She crunched through the mountain snow to the tree and put a hand on its smooth surface. The bark glowed purple beneath her fingers. *Follow your heart,* she thought. Then she realized, *This place is my heart. This whole kingdom is my heart. And this tree—*

Suddenly, the Tree of Ancient Amethyst began to gleam violet and lavender, as if lit from within. Leaves began to flicker to life on its branches.

The sky flashed purple.

Evangeline disappeared.

28

Evangeline opened her eyes. It wasn't like looking in a mirror at all, not in real life. The girl who stood over her, wide-eyed and frowning slightly, might have appeared identical to Evangeline in a photograph, or from a distance, but Evangeline's heart immediately knew the difference.

Images sparked in her brain, lifelong fantasies that had seemed so silly she'd pushed them away or buried them with tears: someone singing with Evangeline in chorus and sitting beside her on the bus; someone whose frayed toothbrush stood next to her own in the juice glass on the bathroom sink. A double birthday cake. No longer was that missing *someone* just a feeling, or a ghost, or a wish—it was a person. It was Desdemona. And it had been Desdemona all along. Evangeline's heart ached as years of gray hollowness were burned away by brilliant joy.

The girl who stood over her now wore diamond earrings and a long velvet cape edged in sapphires. And, of course, she also wore the one thing Evangeline had not found in her room at the palace—a thin golden crown.

"Desdemona!" Evangeline sprang to her feet.

"Evangeline?" The princess stepped closer. She stared, her focused gaze comparing eye color, the twist of a nose, the height of ears. She extended a ringed finger and touched a lock of Evangeline's hair that fell beside her chin. "Is it you? Are you truly real?"

Evangeline nodded. Desdemona's eyes widened. The sisters grinned at each other. Then they giggled. Then they threw their arms around each other and shrieked with laughter.

"How did you get in here?" Desdemona said. "How did you know where to find me?" She leaned against a boulder, cracked in the middle. A majestic purple tree rose high into the forest canopy above them, and Evangeline could hear the splash of a waterfall over her shoulder. Beautiful settees edged in gold and piled with jewel-toned pillows lazed by a sparkling stream. Bookcases laden with rainbows of interesting volumes sprouted from the snow-blanketed ground. And music swirled in the air, just on the edge of Evangeline's hearing.

"I followed my heart," Evangeline said. Desdemona's eyes grew even wider. "And, you know, I had a photograph."

Desdemona laughed, but her face quickly became solemn. "I've waited my whole life to meet you, sister. It's incredible!" She paused. "But now you must leave. At once."

Evangeline's jaw dropped. "What? Look—King Vair is coming for us. The only reason he hasn't snap-frozen both of us is because he couldn't find us. He needed you to find me. Now he knows where we are, and we have to get out of here! I think we can make a mirror portal back to Earth if we work together, but we don't have much time."

"No." Desdemona frowned, lowering herself onto a green velvet footstool. "You must go without me."

Evangeline threw up her hands. What was the matter with her sister? "I came here to help you. You *asked* me for help! The only way we can be safe is by going back—"

"No," Desdemona interrupted quietly. "The king has the rootball stone. I felt it. You must have felt it, too."

Evangeline took a breath. She lowered herself into a cushy blue chair that might have been a giant mushroom. "Yes. He wants to be immortal, because of course he does."

The princess nodded, her expression grave. "That was his plan all along. And he has won. I'm sorry, Evangeline. I should never have let Father convince me to contact you."

"What?" Evangeline thought she must have heard wrong. "That night in the mirror—you did that for *him*?" It wasn't possible, was it? King Vair himself had said Desdemona refused to help him. Evangeline's head was spinning.

Desdemona looked down. The sapphires on her cape cast specks of light all throughout the enchanted wood. "Father told me our mother had been hiding you on Terra for your entire life. I knew he had searched fruitlessly for you. And as I grew older, I felt more and more—I don't know. Connected to you. As though you *should* have been here, but you were missing."

"A space," Evangeline murmured.

Desdemona nodded. She looked at Evangeline with clear eyes. "I knew I could find you. And when Father said he just wanted us to be a family again, I believed him. Despite everything—the missing Keepers, the strange activity at Bright Mine. I wanted to believe him."

Her sister's sad words felt like icicles in Evangeline's chest. "We never expect our parents to lie."

"I didn't know why our mother had been keeping us apart," Desdemona said. "I thought she was just horrible and selfish."

"So did I," Evangeline whispered.

Desdemona shook her head. "I was wrong. She was protecting you from this place. From Father."

Protecting me, Evangeline thought. And for the first time in her life, she wondered if her mother hated boring towns and neutral paint colors as much as Evangeline did. How different would Mom's life have been without the shadow of King Vair always looming over them? A shadow she couldn't even talk about?

Desdemona twined together the fingers that had written frost messages across worlds only a few days ago. "That night in the mirror," she said, "I had every intention of pulling you through, whether you wanted to come or not. I thought it would be for the best. By the time I figured out what Father was really up to, it was too late. You'd found out about me. I'm the reason all this has happened."

Evangeline rose. She couldn't stand to see her sister so defeated. "I'm taking you back with me," she said, her voice hardening. "To Earth. With our mom. We live in a terrible little town called Lakecrest, or Crestlake. I forget. Let Father do what he wants. He'll never find us. We'll live like regular humans."

Desdemona's expression changed. She looked at her sister curiously. "But . . . Evangeline, surely you can't believe we're *humans*."

Evangeline's throat froze. For a moment, she just gaped at her sister. Then she said, "Well, yes. I . . . actually, yes, I thought we were humans. Are we—are we not humans?"

Princess Desdemona rose from her green velvet footstool. Despite everything, she seemed almost amused. Her eyebrows were raised and the corners of her mouth twitched. There was something knowing in her air that reminded Evangeline of their mother, and maybe a little of Sir Paw-on-Stone. "Father is king of the Winter Kingdom,"

Desdemona said. "He's a winterling, of course. And Mother is a summerling. You didn't know that?"

Evangeline suddenly had far more questions than her sister could possibly answer, but all she could sputter was, "Uh, no." She took a deep breath. "Anyway, it doesn't matter. Nobody on Earth will be able to tell."

Now Desdemona's shoulders twisted; she put her hands to her face, and when she took them away again, her eyes shone with emotion. "You don't understand," she cried. "King Vair should never have taken the rootball stone. If he succeeds in awakening the stone, it may give him life, but it will take life from the Winter Kingdom!" The sky over the enchanted forest flashed purple. "You see?" The princess looked stricken. She reached out a hand adorned with jewels and touched Evangeline's fingers. "We can't be together, Evangeline. Not here, and not on Terra. Father never wanted to get rid of us. He wanted to bring us together. We are the children of the Winter and Summer Kingdoms—*we are the only ones who can awaken the rootball stone.*"

Evangeline felt as though the snowy ground were swaying beneath her feet. "You mean—he can't get his immortality without us?"

Desdemona nodded. "King Vair *needs* us. *Both* of us." She smiled sadly. "That's why Mother took you away. That's why we could never be together. The only way to be sure no one ever possessed the power of the rootball stone was to keep us apart."

At that moment, a flash of lightning ripped through the enchanted sky. Both princesses were knocked backward to the forest floor.

A slim figure stepped into the clearing. "I thought I'd find you here, children," King Vair said.

29

The king looked different in this beautiful forest beyond the Tree of Ancient Amethyst, Evangeline realized. In the throne room, flanked by golden-armored guards and trembling servants, he had seemed frighteningly official. Seated on sapphires in his stiff white leather coat and steel circlet, King Vair had fit into the palace like a chandelier in a ballroom—expected, essential, and always above, casting its rays over everyone whether they gazed at it or hid their faces. But here, the king was out of place. His sharp edges and straight lines stuck out, menacing, amongst the snow-dusted trees and worn stones. He looked like an invader.

Evangeline shuddered. She should have felt braver, she knew. She had survived all the dangers the Winter Kingdom had thrown at her so far. But somehow, King Vair was worse than hostile aranae, pointy-helmet guards, even the Lord High Keeper himself. There was something so *calm* about him. A calm lake that covered monsters.

Princess Desdemona's eyes gleamed with surprise. She seemed

unable to move. Exhaling her own fear, Evangeline jumped to her feet, scrambling to put herself between the Winter King and her sister. "Don't come any closer," she snapped.

King Vair cleaned a speck of dirt out from under a clawlike fingernail. "Really, Evangeline. You're being even more ridiculous now than that day in the throne room."

That caught Evangeline off guard. "You—you knew that was me?"

The king advanced, his smile revealing an abundance of white, pointed teeth. "Of course. I knew you at once. What I didn't know was where Desdemona was hiding. She was always clever."

Clever. Nobody had ever called Evangeline clever. Yet here she was, in the Winter Kingdom, with her sister at last. That had to count for something. Evangeline looked at the other princess, who was standing perfectly straight with a frigid scowl on her face.

"I thought I could keep an eye on you in Bright Mine until I succeeded in finding Princess Desdemona," King Vair said. "Imagine my surprise when you escaped—with an arana!" He settled on a luxurious settee nestled next to a mossy stump, throwing his arm over the back. "Oh, I was angry at first." His gray eyes sparked. "But then my spy told me where you were going. The Tree of Ancient Amethyst! Of course, you thought it could protect you." He cocked his head, his black-glass hair shining. "It was sneaky of you to seal the Crystal Gate. It did slow me down." He curled his thin, bluish lips in what could have been a smile. "You should have seen the Lord High Keeper when he realized his portal wouldn't work. I thought his detestable ice face would crack right down the middle."

The king rose, pulling something small from his pocket. "It's time for you to help me, Princesses of the Winter Kingdom. You see, after all these years, the rootball stone is finally mine." He gazed down at the object in his hand. "It has cost me dearly, but it is mine."

Evangeline's body was tense with apprehension, but she couldn't help craning her neck.

The king looked up. "Do you want to see it?" He held the object up between a thumb and forefinger, not quite close enough for Evangeline to touch. It looked a bit like a walnut. She was immediately worried for its safety, balanced precariously between the king's skinny fingers. She wanted to snatch it from his hand.

"That's it?" Desdemona said, a little haughtily.

King Vair's intense gaze was fixed on the drab, walnut-like stone. "That's it. It doesn't look like much, does it? And it isn't. Not right now. But with your help, my dear children, I will awaken it, and call forth life itself. I will unlock the secret to immortality."

Evangeline took a step back. Was there any way to reason with her father? He was looking at the small, dull stone in his hand with wild eyes, like a starving animal. "Don't you care about the Tree of Ancient Amethyst?" she asked. "It's already dying. You can't just steal its life.

You have to return the stone to the rootball where it belongs." She gulped. "We won't help you awaken it."

She looked at Desdemona, who nodded in agreement but didn't speak.

"I don't need your cooperation," King Vair said. "Not now that you're both here. All I need to do is pour your powers into the stone." He slid the rootball stone into his pocket. Then he looked up, that fierce gaze now directed at his two daughters. "Your part is easy. Just . . . hold . . . *still*."

And with that, he lashed out, an electric jet of ice sizzling across the enchanted glen.

"Duck!" Evangeline shouted, and dove into the snow. The large blue mushroom she'd been sitting on earlier crackled, instantly frozen by the king's attack.

"Father, no!" Desdemona cried from behind a branchy bookcase that grew near the bank of the little stream.

Evangeline tried to gather her wits as adrenaline thudded in her ears. *Fight back*, she told herself. *Help me, snow!*

She flung her arms out, casting a snowdrift before her and rolling behind the bookcase where Desdemona was cowering. But King Vair simply waved the drift away with a finger.

Evangeline crouched, her breath heavy. Desdemona looked

shocked. She pressed herself against the back of the bookcase, the sapphires on her velvet cape rattling as she shook.

"Girls," the king called. "It's not too late to help me willingly. Don't make me turn you to ice. You don't really want to be stuck in this enchanted wood forever, do you?"

"You can't trap us in here," Desdemona said. Evangeline could tell she was frightened, but something of her regal attitude couldn't be squelched. Desdemona peeked around the side of the leafy bookcase. "The Tree of Ancient Amethyst will never let you imprison two princesses of the Winter Kingdom!"

A jet of ice sang through the air like the swish of a sharp blade. Desdemona jerked her head back, but the ice caught the corner of her sapphire cape. It instantly froze solid and fell over like a stout tree, dragging the princess with it.

"Desdemona!" Evangeline cried, and reached for her sister, who was kicking her legs against the solid cape. She pulled on the ice clasp as Desdemona wriggled, freeing herself. The princess got to her feet and gathered her skirts, puffy green satin.

"The tree can't help you if it's dead," King Vair called out, a sneer in his voice.

Evangeline flattened herself against the back of the sturdy bookcase. She hadn't even looked at the books it contained. Were they

Desdemona's books? Would she ever find out what her sister liked to read? Her favorite foods? If she liked to swim?

"You'll never awaken the stone," Evangeline barked. "You'll never get our powers." But in spite of her brave words, she felt her shoulders slumping. Where *was* this enchanted forest? Was it all inside the Tree of Ancient Amethyst? What would happen to it when the tree died? In any case, how long could they expect to hide from King Vair now? His gaze had found them. He would not stop until they were both decorations for his ice garden.

For the first time since she'd seen the frost begin to move in her vanity mirror back in Lakecrest, Evangeline felt something heavy curling around her insides, bland and beige and inert. *It's the death of hope*, she realized.

The king's next jet of ice hit the bookcase. With a *SNAP*, branches and shelves and books exploded into chunks of ice, glittering through the air like a firework.

Evangeline and Desdemona gasped. They turned to face King Vair, who stood, hands on white leather hips, at the other end of the enchanted clearing.

Princess Desdemona raised her chin. "The Keepers will never let you do this."

"The Keepers are dead," King Vair said.

Suddenly, out of nowhere, a snooty little voice cut through the air. *"Not all of us."*

Evangeline felt hope stir again. She knew that voice!

With a *crack!*, the enchanted wood disappeared, and suddenly Evangeline was tumbling over snow while wind howled around her.

"Desdemona!" she called through the swirling white flakes.

"Here!" came the voice of her sister.

Evangeline rolled to her knees and found herself face-to-face with golden eyes.

"There you are," Sir Paw-on-Stone said. "Get up, get up! The king is about to have your disheveled little head!"

"What happened? Where are we?" Evangeline asked. It felt like her brain was spinning through stars and dimensions and clam chowder.

The fox looked around. "Where you have been all along. The summit of Bright Mountain. Not all of us can flit between dimensions so easily, of course," he added with a touch of bitterness.

"Get back here!" shouted a voice like a razor. Evangeline saw King Vair shooting lightning jets of ice between the jutting blue stones as Desdemona tried to evade him.

"Sister!" Evangeline screeched as the princess ducked behind a huge crystal. A flash of ice ricocheted off its surface and whizzed past Evangeline's head.

"Over here!" a voice called. Evangeline and Sir Paw-on-Stone slid behind an outcropping. Hortense crouched there, gripping the edge of the tall purple stone with all four hands.

Through the howling of the constant wind and the electric *crack-crack-crack* of King Vair's ice attacks, Evangeline heard a high scream that sounded like her own voice.

But it's not my voice, she thought. It was Desdemona, shrieking as the king struck closer and closer. And even though her sister was a Princess-with-a-capital-*P* and Evangeline wasn't even a member of the Goldfish Club, she realized something. *If our combined powers can awaken the rootball stone, which King Vair can't do*, she thought, *then why couldn't they defeat him?*

Evangeline thrust out her arms. "Come, snow!" she yelled, summoning a veritable avalanche up from the ground. It shot up on all sides of King Vair, who looked surprised in the moment before the snow buried him completely. A second later, the snow exploded and the king was rising to the top, laughing and lashing his ice jets at Princess Desdemona again. But Evangeline's skin flashed ice and her heart thumped strength. *We are stronger than him*, she thought.

"If you won't give me your powers," the king yelled, "I will *take* them!"

Evangeline had to get to her sister. She scooted out from behind her rock shelter and dashed across the cold mountain summit. She could see Desdemona cowering behind the great crystal outcropping, her hands over her face.

Why isn't she fighting back? Evangeline wondered, but was stopped in her tracks by what came out of the snowstorm.

It looked like someone had thrown a greasy lens across the turbulent mountaintop. A portal! Evangeline gasped. A large, dark figure stepped out of the air, followed by a line of red.

It was the Lord High Keeper and a small army of Red Cloaks.

Evangeline was caught in the open. So she sucked in her breath and charged, taking advantage of the fact that the newcomers were disoriented from tumbling out of the portal. She flung snowdrifts as she ran, knocking as many Red Cloaks over as she could. As their feet slipped out from under them and they tumbled forward and backward in the undulating snow, Evangeline had to stop herself from laughing. It was mostly a nervous laugh, a fear laugh, the kind of laugh that pops out at funerals and in dark basements when you're terrified. But a small, *small* part of Evangeline was . . . actually laughing. Before she came to the Winter Kingdom, she would never have imagined that she could protect herself on her own, with her own *real power*. It was exhilarating.

"Desdemona!" she cried, skidding into the snow behind the jutting blue crystal. "I've got an idea."

"Evangeline, what can we do?" Desdemona breathed. She looked frazzled.

Sparrow Fall buzzed around the corner and joined them. "What's going on?" he said, his blue face as pale as a robin's egg.

"Sparrow Fall!" Evangeline said. "I need you to do something for me. Something very brave."

The fairy nervously expelled a puff of glitter, but he nodded. "I can do it."

"Good." Evangeline gave him an encouraging smile. "Get Hortense and Sir Paw-on-Stone," she said. "They have to keep the Lord High Keeper and his Red Cloaks busy while Princess Desdemona and I deal with King Vair."

Sparrow Fall's eyes grew as wide as blueberries, but he didn't argue. He just set his jaw, nodded, and flew off.

Evangeline turned to her sister. "Okay, listen. We've got to work together. That's our only chance. That's the only way we can beat the king. We have to combine our powers."

The look on her sister's face stopped Evangeline short. "I...," Desdemona said. "I don't have any powers."

"What?" Evangeline gaped. She slumped back on her knees. "You are a princess of the Winter Kingdom!" she cried. "Of course you have powers! How did you travel through the Crystal Gate? How did you get inside the Tree of Ancient Amethyst?"

"I had help from a Keeper. Madam Walks-Through-Walls." Desdemona fell back against the purple rock as jets of ice exploded around them. "I've never been able to use powers. I've never really needed to."

"Well, you need to now," Evangeline said. Behind them, she could hear the frustrated cries of the Lord High Keeper and his Red Cloaks, and, occasionally, the buzz of tiny wings, the *pop!* of a portal being thrown into existence, or the terrifying hiss of a ticked-off arana.

Desdemona looked as though she were going to cry. Evangeline stared at her sister's face, like wax that was softening, framed by diamond earrings and a golden crown. As soon as she'd found out about her twin, Evangeline had imagined someone to fill the space and hold her up. But maybe princesses needed to be held up sometimes, too.

"Hey," Evangeline said, her voice as strong as she could make it. "You're the one who noticed the extra miners. You're the one who was suspicious about the disappearing Keepers, and escaped Father, and kept yourself safe. And *you're* the one who found *me*, across mirrors and worlds."

"None of that was magic," Desdemona said with a sniff.

Evangeline frowned, thinking. "I don't really know what magic is," she said. "But I know that this is *your* kingdom. And it will listen to you." She took her sister's hand. "I promise."

Desdemona smiled hesitantly, but nodded. "Okay."

"Now," Evangeline said, tensing the muscles in her legs and pulling Desdemona away from the shelter of the purple crystal, "on the count of three, we charge. Throw everything you've got at him. It's two against one." She gave her sister as fierce a look as she could muster. "Are you ready?"

The princess nodded.

"One . . . two . . . *three!*"

With a cry, the two princesses of the Winter Kingdom raced across the summit of Bright Mountain. One of King Vair's jets glanced off Evangeline's shoulder, but she kept running, casting snow, ice, wind, and the rage of the ravaged land at its treacherous ruler. The breath of the Winter Kingdom gushed into Evangeline's pores and balled itself in her fingertips, at her elbows, behind her eyes. *Ready*, it whispered.

"Now!" Evangeline yelled. She pointed and punched into the air, directing the snow, casting everything she had at the wicked figure in white leather who lashed out from the peak.

Suddenly, she felt a surge of power from just over her right shoulder. Evangeline glanced back to see her sister launch a mountain's worth of winter at the king, her hair flying.

"Go, Desdemona!" Evangeline whooped.

At last, King Vair couldn't fight off the snow and ice any longer. His movements slowed as Evangeline and Desdemona kept coming. Then he froze. Not entirely, but enough. Evangeline felt ice coursing through her veins, twining around the king, weaving itself with Desdemona's magic. She tried to keep focus, focus, *focus*.

And then—she began to get tired. It was like trying to hold her fingers closed around a metal ball that just kept expanding. "No!" she yelped, losing her grip.

"Two princesses of the Winter Kingdom," King Vair said. He couldn't move his body, but he was regaining his strength. "And of the Summer Kingdom. The only ones who can awaken the rootball stone, which answers to two masters. How I wanted to rule beside my daughters."

"What?" Desdemona said, letting her arms fall.

"No!" Evangeline called, breathing heavily now. "Don't let go!"

"What do you mean, rule beside us?" Desdemona took a step toward her father.

"What good is immortality if you have no one to share it with?" King Vair said, struggling against Evangeline's hold and winning, inch by inch. "I would grant it to you, and to Evangeline. Think of the peace we could bring to the Winter Kingdom, for all time."

Desdemona took another step. "Do you really want that?"

The king nodded. Then, with a cracking sound, he broke free, casting two ferocious jets of ice, one at each princess. Desdemona and Evangeline were stuck, with only their heads free.

"No!" Evangeline wriggled, but her limbs were frozen and wouldn't respond. She twisted her neck to find the summit littered with Red Cloaks nursing wounds. Hortense had crawled under a rock, Sir

Paw-on-Stone lay quite still in a depression in the snow, and Sparrow Fall was nowhere to be seen.

"Now, let's get this over with." The king held up the small, walnutty object—the remarkable rootball stone. "I finally have you two in the same place at the same time."

He traced a shape in the air. Suddenly, sparks began shooting from the rootball stone. Not white sparks, but flashes of black and brown and green. Evangeline could feel them on her skin. They were sharp and angry, and they seemed to be sucking all her energy, maybe even her life, out of her pores. Her eyelids grew heavy.

"The princesses of summer and winter," the king was saying. "For as I am King of the Winter Kingdom, so your mother was Queen of the Summer Kingdom."

Just then, a flash of brilliant green lit the mountaintop like a lightning strike, leaving a shimmering portal in the air. And as King Vair watched, agape, a vision of sparkling blue stepped through.

"Yes, I was Queen of Summer," Evangeline's mother said, her hands on the hips of her remarkable blue gown. "And that's the only reason you ever wanted to marry me."

30

"Rose!" King Vair said. His voice was jovial, but Evangeline sensed something else underneath. "You never visit."

"You are *still* chasing this—this *fantasy*," the woman in the blue gown said. Evangeline stared at her mother's face, glowing and beautiful in the brilliant winter light. Mom's face wasn't hiding anything anymore, and Evangeline saw her for who she was. Who she had always been. A queen. Watching her now, chin held high and eyes flashing, Evangeline couldn't imagine how her mother could ever have kept it a secret.

The queen lifted her glittering blue skirt a few inches and stepped lightly over the body of a Red Cloak who lay moaning in the snow. "These are your children!" she said, her voice severe.

"And you have kept one of them from me for almost twelve years!" the king spat.

Rose pursed her lips. "I had to," she said. Then she added, softer, "I'm sorry."

At first, Evangeline couldn't believe her mother would ever apologize to this horrible, power-mad king. But when she looked, she was surprised to find the queen was actually speaking to Desdemona.

Desdemona scowled and turned her face away.

"I'm sorry," Rose said again. "Desdemona. I missed you every moment of every day."

Desdemona said nothing. The queen flicked her wrist, and the ice holding the two princesses disintegrated into sparkling golden dust. She moved toward her daughters. "By the time I figured out how obsessed your father was with the blasted rootball stone, it was too late," the queen said. "I knew you girls could never be together. Never ever. Not here, not on Earth. If you were together, he could harness the stone's power." She sighed. "Which was all he ever cared about."

King Vair pointed at her. "That's not true."

"Yes," Rose said, "it is."

The king scowled. "You're jealous you don't have the rootball stone for yourself. And you never will!" In a flash, he thrust the stone into the air again. It sparked in his grip, and Evangeline felt despair crawling through the roots below her feet.

Then a frigid blast knocked her off balance. She felt like she had been punched in the stomach. She fell to the ground as Desdemona crumpled next to her.

"Fight him, Evangeline! Desdemona!" their mother cried, rushing forward as the king tossed savage ice jets at her with his free hand.

Evangeline watched her mother winding through King Vair's ice attacks on a golden spring wind, rising and falling and casting bubbles of green light before her. She looked like a shot-putter from the Olympics, grunting as she hurled energy toward the flailing Winter King. One of the green balls of light collided with a jet of ice and exploded, shattering a jutting rock nearby.

Evangeline tried to get up, but she could barely keep her eyes open. The black sparks were all around her, digging into her skin.

But she managed to reach out a hand, fingers probing the snow next to her where she knew her sister was lying. Slowly she scratched, searching, as her head grew heavier. At last, she found Desdemona's hand. It was still and cold. But after a moment, the fingers began to twitch. Evangeline grasped. The sisters squeezed hands.

And that little movement, that tiny expression of solidarity, seemed to awaken Evangeline again. She felt the snow underneath her, let it seep into her blood. She pushed away the black sparks. Next to her, Desdemona was stirring as well.

Evangeline crawled to her knees. Then she got to her feet, extending a hand and pulling Princess Desdemona up with her. They exchanged quick smiles, and Evangeline felt the black sparks receding and strength flowing back into her arms.

But Queen Rose was getting tired. With a great cry, she threw a massive ball of green light toward the king, but he leapt out of the way and swung around, throwing an ice jet back that blasted through a tall snowdrift.

And hit the queen squarely in the gut.

Evangeline's mother had only a second to gasp before she was frozen solid.

"Mother!" Desdemona cried, and began to run. "Mother, I'm sorry! I forgive you! I forgive you!"

"Wait!" Evangeline tried to grab her sister's arm, but she slipped away, racing headlong toward the ice statue of Queen Rose in her sparkling gown.

King Vair flung a hand in Desdemona's direction, and his ice beam struck her in the back. She froze instantly, arms outstretched.

"Desdemona!" Evangeline cried.

Now the king turned to Evangeline. "I didn't want to do this," he said. "But I have to." And he lifted his hand.

Evangeline glared at him, ice crackling under her fingernails. She was alone. Everything dear to her had been stripped away, and now it was just her and King Vair, face-to-face on this howling mountaintop. She was electric with anger.

But beyond herself, in the wind and under the soles of her feet, she felt something else: *betrayal*. She felt the guts and bones of this frozen world heaving with fury. She felt a distant wailing that rattled her teeth, and the bleak emptiness of the hole left by the rootball stone. King Vair had ripped something precious from its deep, secret nest and the trees didn't like it. The land didn't like it.

"Goodbye, Evangeline," King Vair said. And with a great *swish* of his hand, an arc of ice spikes burst forth, flying at Evangeline like arrows from a bow.

But she didn't wince, or close her eyes. She was a calm lake, with nothing below the surface but deep, deep water. She took a step forward. Three ice jets struck her at full force, *THWACK-THWACK-THWACK*.

And melted away, as though they were nothing more than cotton candy in her mouth.

King Vair's jaw dropped in shock. He looked down at his hand.

Evangeline crossed her arms over her chest. Then, in a single, decisive motion, she thrust them down to her sides. *WHOOSH!* The ground trembled like the growl of a great beast, sending snow and crystal and hunks of blue stone into the air.

The king put his hands over his head, trying to duck the debris and keep his footing. He staggered for a moment, arms flailing and off-balance.

Then, out of nowhere, a rainbow blur smacked him square in the chest. The king fell onto his back in the snow. The rootball stone rolled from his fingers, and in an instant, the rainbow blur had swooped down and grabbed it.

"Sparrow Fall!" Evangeline said as the fairy alighted on her shoulder. "*That* was very brave of you."

"You, too," he said.

31

In some ways, the palace of the Winter Kingdom hadn't changed at all since the last time Evangeline was here. The towering white walls still whispered opalescent ripples, the blue-armored guards with the clawed axes still stood in neat rows, and the brass candelabras shone softly in the long hallways.

But one thing was different. As Evangeline followed her mother and sister down a wide marble staircase, trying with all her might to have *half* the perfect posture they did, she felt something she had never felt in her life. *This place could be home.*

It wasn't quite home yet. But as they made their way through what used to be the ice sculpture garden, and was now just the regular garden, she could imagine herself spending an afternoon next to the little pond with a good book—maybe a mystery, which Desdemona didn't care for—or learning how to grow strange, yellow-spotted apples.

Queen Rose stopped outside the door to the blue throne room. "You girls can sit up high, in the gallery." She set her mouth in a slightly worried way that reminded Evangeline of the old days. "If you still insist on watching."

The twins exchanged a look, then both nodded at their mother. Evangeline had wondered if it would be too much for Desdemona to watch King Vair be accused of his crimes before the whole kingdom, but she was just as resolved as Evangeline herself.

"Very well." Queen Rose put a ringed hand on the princesses' shoulders. "I'll see you afterward, my dears. Don't forget—tonight is Hortense's first concert as Royal Violinist. You won't want to miss our duet."

"We'll be there, Mother," Desdemona said.

"Wouldn't miss it," Evangeline added.

The queen smiled. Then she nodded to the fish-eyed page boy, who bowed low and opened the narrow door to the gallery stairs.

❋ ❋ ❋

"Vair of Rime Village," the queen's stern voice echoed from atop the sapphire throne. "You stole the precious rootball stone from its rightful place between the Winter and Summer Kingdoms, nearly causing irreparable harm to the Trees of Ancient Amethyst and Topaz."

The thin man in chains at the center of the vast blue throne room said nothing.

"You are also accused, along with your Lord High Keeper, of secretly arranging the deaths of ten Keepers of the Crystal Gate."

"You can't prove that," rumbled a sullen ice troll who was chained next to the thin man.

Evangeline's mother leaned back in the throne. "No," she said. "We cannot." She looked around the cavernous room. Many citizens of the Winter Kingdom had gathered. "But we have proof that you inflicted many cruel punishments on your subjects."

From her seat in the balcony next to Princess Desdemona, Princess Evangeline's gaze moved from the fish-eyed page boy to a group of whispering aranae to an old man who sat quietly near the door with his beloved violin.

The ice troll grunted, but Evangeline's father didn't say a word.

"All in pursuit of a power that should never have been yours," Rose said. "That should never belong to anyone." She paused.

"So what are you going to do?" the former Lord High Keeper said, a bit cautiously. "Your Majesty."

The queen considered this for a moment. Then she said, "You are banished to Earth, where you can cause no more trouble."

"What! Live among the humans!" the former Lord High Keeper exclaimed. "I'm an *ice troll*! He's a winterling! Impossible!"

The queen sat back in her tall throne. "It is completely possible, I assure you. And we shall disguise you, of course." She gestured to one of her golden-armored bodyguards. "Escort these gentlemen from the palace, and have the Center of Dark Light prepare them a mirror portal to Terra." She gave one last, almost wistful look to the thin man in chains. "I do not wish to see either of them again. That is all."

The queen rose and descended the throne steps as the crowd dispersed. In the gallery, Hortense leaned over to Evangeline. "Are you going to stay here, then?"

Evangeline nodded. "My mom belongs here. I don't think she was ever suited to life on Earth. And my grandma will be here soon. She's going to live in the Summer Kingdom with my aunt, though." She sighed. "I don't know. It's great here, but sometimes I think the whole princess life just isn't really my thing."

"I agree with you there," Desdemona said, fanning herself with a delicate lace fan. *It's still great to have a sister*, Evangeline thought. It was the best thing in the world. But . . . sometimes Desdemona could be kind of annoying.

"You could help me," Sir Paw-on-Stone said. He was gazing at the crowd below through a little monocle that made him look far more adorable than Evangeline would ever dare tell him. "I have to start recruiting and training new Keepers."

"I think helping the Lord High Keeper would be a great use of your time, sweetie," came a voice from behind them. Queen Rose ruffled Evangeline's hair. "He's going to start with the fairies. And may I just say that Sparrow Fall seems like an excellent candidate."

The fairy appeared from nowhere, as he seemed to do. "Me?" he squeaked. "Oh, no. No, no, no. Keepers' jobs are much too dangerous. How about my brother?"

"We shall see," said Sir Paw-on-Stone. With his fancy new title of "Lord High Keeper," Evangeline thought he was getting even snootier.

"I think Taranta Lily would be a good Keeper," Hortense said, "since Your Majesty has graciously reinstated the position of Arana Keeper." She blushed.

"Taranta Lily would be a fine choice," the queen said, leaning against the balcony railing, the light from the tall windows glinting off her blue ball gown. "But, as it happens, the aranae already have a Keeper. His name is Pink."

"What?" Hortense said in surprise. "But—he was executed!"

The queen smiled. "It turns out he was in hiding. Disguised as a bartender in a remote little village."

"What village?" Evangeline asked.

"Oak," said the queen.

Sparrow Fall spat glitter all over the balcony in astonishment. "Well, knock me over with a feather."

"Easily done, I should think," Sir Paw-on-Stone muttered.

Evangeline leaned back in her seat, her mother's hand warm on her shoulder. She was a princess—a princess! Princess Evangeline.

But, to her surprise, it didn't make her feel that much different than she had in Crestlake—or was it Lakecrest? She thought about the rows of sparkly dresses hanging in her huge closet, the selection of audacious tiaras in her jewelry armoire, and the exquisite crystal violin Hortense had unsuccessfully been trying to teach her how to play (so far, Evangeline's entire repertoire was a version of "Twinkle, Twinkle, Little Star" that sounded more like "These Alley Cats Are Very Angry"). But none of those beautiful things caused the electric tingle in her chest that happened as she looked around the crowded balcony at the now-familiar faces who were gathered there. Sir Paw-on-Stone, with his new, even purpler cape; Desdemona, so much like Evangeline yet so different, who had been missing for so long; Sparrow Fall, and the way he still cast secret, puppy-eyed glances at Hortense; and dear Hortense herself, Evangeline's first real friend.

Evangeline slouched in her velvet chair as the sounds of the palace of the Winter Kingdom swirled around her. Being a princess was nothing compared to being a friend.

Acknowledgments

Thank you to Ammi-Joan Paquette, Mallory Kass, and my mom and dad.

ABOUT THE AUTHOR

Adi Rule is the author of *The Hidden Twin* and *Strange Sweet Song*. She lives in a New Hampshire swamp with three cats who barely tolerate one another. Visit her online at adirule.com.